Zachary is ready now for the final release, the showing of emotions. Just as Clara had done. "All my life," he says, "I've never had a single fight with my mom. Do you know why? I mean, I need to discuss this with Nancy, but I think it's because I'm *scared* of Mom. I think when I was a little boy, I got the idea she was ruthless because of what she did to Dad. I thought, if you pissed her off, she could just call the cops and have you taken away! I thought she might do that to me. I was . . . like muzzled. That's why I forgot everything. Because I was scared. I've always felt guilty around her, like she doesn't love me as much as Josh. See why? Because I betrayed her to go with Dad. When I think about it . . ." He pauses to gather and feel his own anger. ". . . what she did was *despicable*! She let those cops beat my father up right in front of me! She deprived me of my father the whole time I was growing up just to be vindictive! She lied to me about my own life! All these years she's just . . . lied!"

THE TIGER ORCHARD

Joyce Sweeney

Published by
Bantam Doubleday Dell Books for Young Readers
a division of
Bantam Doubleday Dell Publishing Group, Inc.
1540 Broadway
New York, New York 10036

The trademark Laurel-Leaf Library® is registered in the U.S.
Patent and Trademark Office.
The trademark Dell® is registered in the U.S. Patent
and Trademark Office.

ISBN: 0-440-21927-2

RL: 5.3

Reprinted by arrangement with Delacorte Press

Printed in the United States of America

February 1995

10 9 8 8 7 6 5 4 3 2 1

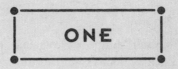

ONE

The smell of gasoline. So strong and so sweet. Is he hanging upside down? Then something silver running by, very fast. Yards of silver satin. Ice, maybe. The Man's voice says, "It's only fair . . ." Zachary looks at himself in a mirror. A tiny little mirror. Four years old, blond, freckles, hair blowing in the wind. "Hey!" says the Man, and the mirror disappears.

Then there are trees, tall scary trees like in *The Wizard of Oz*, throwing apples, but they get past that.

Then they, Zachary and the Man, are in a car, pulling up in front of the house where Zachary used to live. "Wait here," says the Man, and he goes up the steps and into the house.

Zachary is scared for the Man. He's worried. The Man doesn't come back. They're hurting him in there. Zachary has to go to the bathroom. He doesn't like to disobey, but the house is so quiet and he doesn't want to wait. He wants to see if the Man is all right.

The house is silent. Zachary climbs the porch steps and opens the door. The knob is high and hard to turn. He goes into the living room. There's no one there. It's a trap. Then he sees it in the shadows. A Bengal tiger big as

1

a car, walking slowly forward, gazing at Zachary. Coming to eat him.

He feels himself jump back against the door. It's latched and Zachary doesn't want to turn around to work the latch. He's scared of the tiger. It's coming to get him. It's coming to eat him, and Zachary tries to scream, but no scream comes out . . .

"Zack! Zack! Hey. It's a dream. It's a dream."

Joshua. Joshua. Always at the end of a nightmare there's poor Josh having to wake him up. Zachary breathes deeply until he's not a little boy anymore but an eighteen-year-old, in a safe suburban bedroom with his sixteen-year-old brother. And no tigers in sight. In the dim light he focuses on Joshua's sweet, virginal face and mussed hair. "It's okay, man," Joshua says, gently prying Zack's fingers from his arm, where they're cutting off the circulation. "It was just a dream."

"Okay," Zack pants. He tries so hard to breathe correctly, he almost wears himself out. "It's okay now. Thanks."

Josh pats him gently. "Anytime."

He means it. Josh is a saint; so patient night after night, getting his sleep disturbed because Zachary has a problem. Zack is the only problem person in the house. Josh and Mom have no problems. They cook dinner together in peaceful silence, like robots. They play piano duets. Zack, with his bad dreams and messy hobbies, stands out.

But Josh is philosophical. He's back in bed now, cuddling down under his spread like a contented baby. Ready to continue his dreams about, what? Maybe musical notes falling around him like autumn leaves. Something gentle like that. Josh has a normal mind. He's no trouble at all.

Zack is trouble. Not that you can tell from his high grade point average or his neat closets and drawers. When he leaves for school in a T-shirt and jeans, there are no outward signs. No one in the senior class at Taravella knows. They think he's a good guy. He's more popular than Josh. Better at sports. Better with girls.

But here at home they know. Josh knows. Mom knows. Nancy, the psychologist, knows. And Zack knows. And that's why he has to stay awake now while Josh sleeps, and turn on the flashlight by his bed and write down the whole dream in a notebook, like those old-fashioned punishments where they make a kid write something a hundred times until he's brainwashed.

•

Fourth period is a sanctuary. The Temple of Art. That's Mr. Taylor's joke. If there's too much talking and giggling, he raises his perfect eyebrows and says, "Frivolity in the Temple of Art?" He's a nice guy; knows how to laugh at himself. He's brave. Zack thinks it's brave to be an art teacher. Sometime in his life Mr. Taylor must have wanted to be a real painter with shows and galleries, but it didn't happen. It takes guts, Zachary thinks, to help other people get what you missed out on.

Zack needs inspiration. They're supposed to be doing pencil portraits of one another. Mr. Taylor said pick a student who inspires you and draw the inner person. Nobody inspires Zack. He pretends to fuss with his equipment, scanning the room, looking for an inner person that doesn't make him sick. Mr. Taylor looks inspiring, but that would be a bad idea. Zack watches them all, sitting at strange angles to one another, their sketch pads turning into little mirrors of what's going on in the room. It's like an M. C. Escher drawing. Maybe Zack could do that. No, that's not the assignment. Pick some*one*. Focus on a personality. Zack decides he doesn't like anyone in his art class well enough to spend talent on them. He decides to bring this up with Nancy tonight. Maybe he's antisocial.

Zack is saved by an interruption. The door opens and a strange girl comes into the art room. Zack is inspired. She's wearing three shades of purple; that's the first thing he notices. Her blouse is blue-purple, like lilacs. Her jeans are violet. Around her waist is a band of magenta. Her hair is short and dark and curly, and she has the sweet, valentine face of Spanish and Italian girls. She's short and just a little chubby. All circles. She goes to Mr. Taylor's desk and leans over it, handing him a note. Her violet jeans are snug. Zack has bad thoughts in the Temple of Art.

Mr. Taylor stands up. "If I might break into your divine inspiration for a moment. We have a new student. Clarissa Benedetto."

4

She has faced the class now, presenting her valentine face and the swell of her lilac blouse. Zack's heart is singing opera. Clarissa Benedetto! Clarissa Benedetto!

"Clarissa is from East Orange, New Jersey," Mr. Taylor says. He turns to Clarissa. "You'll feel right at home here in South Florida."

Everyone laughs but Clarissa, who doesn't know what he means. But she doesn't seem to care, either. She's scanning the room, looking at the kids. Zack is impressed. Most new kids die a thousand deaths under scrutiny. But Clarissa Benedetto is scrutinizing everyone right back.

Mr. Taylor gives her a sketch pad. "Look around the room and find someone who inspires you and make a sketch that reveals the inner person."

Clarissa scans again. She looks directly at Zack.

Yes, yes, mi amore, he encourages her silently.

She walks over and sits down on the floor near him. She smells like lilacs.

Zack is overjoyed but not surprised. People are often attracted to him. In classes teachers lecture to him, comforted by his steady gaze. When he sits in a bus shelter, strangers invariably strike up conversations with him. He always thought that trait was a nuisance, but finally it has paid off. "I'm glad you came over," he says, choosing his pencil. "I couldn't find anybody to draw."

"That's why I chose you," she says. "You looked so lonely over here."

Zack is angry. Was that an insult? He doesn't want her pity! She should see that if he's off in a corner by himself it's because he wants it that way. He would tell her so, too, but she intimidates him. He feels she's maybe psychic or something; has some way of knowing his worst secrets, like the fact that he's hot for her, or that he's concealing insanity. Zack decides not to talk. Whenever he's in doubt, he holds still and does nothing.

"What's your name?" she asks, cocking her head back to look at him.

"Zachary."

"That's a good name," she says, beginning to sketch. "Do you like to be called Zack?"

"Yes," he says carefully. "Do you like to be called Clare?"

"No. I like to be called Clarissa. I let a few people call me Clara, but only really special people."

Zack feels she is telling him *he* will never be one of those people. He feels the most peculiar sense of loss, as if he'd missed an important train. Then he thinks how truly crazy he has become. She's a total stranger and she's jerking his emotions like puppet strings.

Now she's staring at him. "You aren't drawing," she says.

She has pushed him so far, he's almost angry. "I'm having trouble with you," he says coldly. "You're a difficult type."

She laughs. "Leave my personality out of it."

It's a magical incantation. They both laugh and the barrier between them shatters. "That's okay," Zack says. "I'm a difficult type too."

6

Clarissa Benedetto sucks her pencil. "In that case we better stick together."

·

He rides home on clouds, elated. Even being crazy isn't so bad now. Nothing will really ever be bad again. Trees are better, grass is better. Zack nears his yard and sees his golden retriever, Sunbeam, on the lawn. It's enough to make him weep. He kneels down and lets the dog run to him and vault into his embrace. "Beamer," he chants, snuggling sun-heated fur. "My best, best, best, best boy. My sweetie-honey-boy." Sunbeam feels the same way, is licking and struggling against Zack's body as if he wanted to push through to the other side. Zack always lavishes love on Beamer, but it's even worse today because he has to get rid of his excess love for Clarissa Benedetto. "Big, blond baby," he tells the dog solemnly. They hold the embrace a long time. Beamer is Zack's dog more than Joshua's because Zack pays more attention to him. Joshua's love is restrained and universal. Zack's is intense and specific. Joshua pats Beamer and says "Good dog." He would never stoop to a phrase like "sweetie-honey-boy."

"I'm in love, buddy," Zack tells his dog. "Don't tell a soul. We blonds have to stick together." That's an old joke. Zack feels a little left out because Josh and Mom are so alike. Zack joked once that the only person in the family he looked like was the dog, but Mom didn't think it was funny. "Her name is Clarissa Benedetto," he continues, leading the dog toward the house. "Wait till you see her. She's like a Botticelli angel. Are you hungry?"

They go inside. The house is deserted because it's Wednesday. On Wednesday Josh has orchestra practice, Mom goes to the grocery, and later Zack has therapy. So they make no effort to eat a family dinner. Zack loves Wednesdays. He and Beamer share a few Twinkies, and Zack tells the dog all about Clarissa Benedetto. "We're going to fall in love," he explains. "She's going to let me call her Clara, and we're going to— Well, you're too young to hear what else. You should have seen the drawing she did of me. She likes me. I should have asked her to eat lunch with me, but I chickened out. I'm going to tomorrow, though. Do you think I should dump Tracy?" Tracy was Zack's current, unofficial girlfriend.

Beamer tilts his head, several times, considering the angles. Then he barks.

"You're right. I'm going to do it. Clear the field."

Zack picks up the phone and dials.

"Hello?" Tracy says.

"Hi. It's me."

Instantly coy. "Hi, Me."

Suddenly Zack hates her. "I've been thinking . . ."

Coy switches to wary. "About what?"

"About us." He glances at the dog, who ducks his head. Wary to hostile. "Oh?"

"We're getting into a rut, aren't we?"

"Are we?"

"Going through the motions. You know?"

"What are you trying to say, Zachary?"

Bitch. He hates her. She's in his way. "I think we should see other people."

A calculated silence. "I don't think I want to see you at all on those terms."

He glances at the dog again. "Okay."

"Okay, what?" She didn't expect that.

"Okay, good-bye."

"Just like that?" She sounds really upset.

He could kill her. Who does she think she is, making him feel guilty? "I guess so."

She hangs up on him. Manipulating *and* rude! What did he ever see in her? But now that she's gone he feels horrible. "I'm a bad person, Sunbeam," he says to the dog. "I'm the worst. I'm a coldhearted bastard. It would serve me right if Clarissa won't have me and I end up all alone."

He feels exhausted. He's glad it's therapy night. Nancy will fix this. Maybe.

Beamer suddenly runs into the living room. A second later the door opens. "Is anybody here?" his mother calls.

"Yes." Zack gets up and rushes in quickly in case she needs his help.

Mary Lloyd is a pretty woman. She looks like Joshua with her round, trusting eyes and soft brown hair. She's the kind of woman everyone rushes to help and everyone admires—a widow, raising two boys alone, holding down a job, keeping a house up. She's a saint. When Zack first discussed his mother with Nancy and explained how wonderful she was, Nancy said, "You must be holding back something big."

Zack looks for signs of disappointment that *he's* the one home, but he sees none. "Hello," she says. "The bags are in the car."

He hurries to get them, Beamer at his side. When he comes back, laden down, she is in the kitchen, looking in the pantry cupboard.

"Mom, you got plastic again," he says patiently.

"What?"

"They give you a choice of paper or plastic bags for the groceries. You should ask for paper."

"Oh, yes. I forgot. These are so much easier to carry."

With difficulty he swallows his environmental lecture. They are alone so rarely. He distracts himself by putting groceries away.

"Have you eaten?" she asks. "Are you hungry?"

"I had some Twinkies with the dog."

She turns and looks at him disapprovingly. But she doesn't say anything. She isn't that kind of mom. "I'm going to have some vegetable soup," she says.

Zack hates vegetable soup. "Me too."

They eat in silence. Every few seconds they pause to crumble crackers. "Your brother is late tonight," she says wistfully.

"That concert is Friday night," he reminds her. "They have to get ready."

"Oh! That's right! That's going to be wonderful."

Zack wants something comparable. "It's only a month till graduation," he says.

"Time flies," she agrees. "Did anything interesting happen to you today?"

"No," he says. "Same old stuff." Then he wonders what in hell is wrong with him. He fell in *love* today. He broke up with his girlfriend and now feels terrible about it. When Nancy asks what's going on, he knows he will pour all that out. But when his own mother asked, it was almost as if he couldn't remember. No wonder they aren't as close as he'd like them to be! Maybe it's all his fault. He gathers his courage and really starts to tell her, but now she's looking at a seed catalogue that came in the mail and he hates to disturb her.

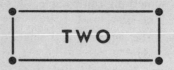

TWO

"What does gasoline mean to you?" Nancy reaches for her cigarettes, probably as bored with this as Zack. How can you trust a therapist who smokes?

"Dollar forty-nine for regular," Zack says. Then he feels ashamed. They've already covered using flippancy as a mask, but it comes so easily to him.

Nancy gives him a brief, baleful stare and pushes back her messy hair. "In the context of this dream, what do you think the smell of gasoline might mean?" She lights up and blows out smoke like a pool hustler. Zack wonders if she is really listening or if she does all this stuff unconsciously.

"Dangerous," he says. "You know, like when they tie the hero up and start pouring gasoline over him."

"Better," she says, making a note. "This is a scary dream for sure. The apple trees are attacking you, and that tiger, for God's sake. This man you're with, though. Is he scary or do you like him?"

Zack has to think. "Both."

"What does he look like?"

"I can't see him."

"Yes, you can. Concentrate."

"No, I can't see him. He's like a shadow."

"Literally?"

Zack loses his concentration. "I don't know."

"What do apple trees mean to you?"

"I like them." He shifts in his chair. He doesn't like her chairs.

She writes this down. "Why?"

He is suddenly sick of all this. "Who *doesn't* like apple trees?"

She stops writing and gives him a tough-girl stare. She is so unlike the sweet, warm therapists of television. Zack had pictured himself getting somebody like Robert Young, who would pat his hand and tell him it's okay to cry. Instead he got Nancy Kline, an anorexic chain-smoker who glares at him and challenges every word he says. Still, in a funny way Zack likes it. No one has ever treated him like this before. It makes him feel important just to know he can actually piss someone off. She glares at him a long time for effect, then sits back like she might really be giving up on him. She looks up at the ceiling. "It's your money, junior," she concludes.

Shamed, he makes a true effort. "I've always liked the feeling of apples and apple trees. It's one of the reasons I don't like Florida. Up north you get this magical feeling in the fall, in October, when everybody puts ghosts in their trees and jack-o'-lanterns on their porches."

"People do that here."

"It's not the same! The air doesn't smell like fall here.

In Ohio you could drive around and see these roadside stands out in the country where they sell apple cider and doughnuts . . ."

"Did you do that every year?" she asks. "With your family?"

"No. You just drive by and *see* them. I never— I don't think our family ever stopped at one. I . . ." Suddenly he feels really confused. "Maybe when I was really little or something. Anyway, it's a wonderful feeling you can't get in the tropics. All we have here is the goddam *lobster* season. It's not the same."

"We keep going back to Ohio and your childhood," she says. "You dreamed about your old house. You saw yourself in some kind of mirror as a little boy. Now you're telling me the apples here aren't as good as in Ohio, or some such stuff. I think more and more we're dealing with a memory here. What's back in Ohio you want to retrieve?"

"I can hardly remember that time. We moved when I was five."

"If you can hardly remember it, how can you be sure how wonderful the autumn was?"

"It's just a vague feeling."

"Uh-huh. Okay, let's take a crack at the tiger and then we'll spend some time in the real world, shall we?"

"With pleasure," Zack said. He hates dream analysis. He wants to talk about Clarissa.

"What do tigers mean to you?"

He suppresses the urge to say "Clemson." "Big, scary,

14

but friendly too. Like Tigger. Or Tony the Tiger. I guess I like tigers."

"You didn't like the one in the dream, did you?"

"Yes, I did, in a way. I mean I was scared, but I was fascinated too. I wanted . . ."

"Don't stop now!"

"I wanted to win him over. I felt like . . . it wasn't *his* fault. Somebody let him out. Oh, I don't know. I'm just making stuff up to please you now."

"Are you?" She crushes out her cigarette. On her desk is a sign that says THANK YOU FOR NOT MENTIONING MY SMOK-ING. "What do you think happened to the man who went into the house?" she asks. "Did he turn into the tiger?"

"No," Zack says. "He's dead. The tiger ate him. That's — I feel so bad because . . . if I'd gone with him, maybe the tiger wouldn't have hurt him. I feel bad. I almost feel like it would be only fair if the tiger would get me too. I should have stayed with the man."

She leans forward, suddenly. "Who is that man, Zack?"

They hold each other's eyes. His body is rigid from effort. Then he slumps. "I don't know." He feels like he's going to cry.

"Don't panic." She closes his dream diary and slides it across the desk to him. "Rome wasn't built in a day. How was school today?"

He perks up. "I fell in love."

She laughs. She's nicer when they aren't working on

dreams. "That hardly ever happens to eighteen-year-old boys!" she says. "What's she like?"

"You know Raphael's *Madonna*?"

She guffaws, slapping at the edge of the desk. "Good thing for you I don't put much stock in Freud!"

He laughs too. "Her name is Clarissa Benedetto. She says she lets special people call her Clara."

"Sounds like an operator."

"No! She's very honest. She seems like she has a lot of integrity."

"Don't decide that if you just met her today. When I first met you, I thought you were basically honest. We both know better now."

He never knows how to take these playful insults. He feels bad about not being honest with himself. He can't see why she wants to tease him about it. "You're not honest either!" he points out. "You're always trying to trick me."

"I trick you into being honest," she says. "Don't worry about *my* job. Just do your job. So did you hit it off with her?"

"I think so. It's hard to tell. I think I'll ask her to eat lunch with me tomorrow."

"Do it," she agrees. "Do you like her better than Tracy?"

He hangs his head. "I broke up with Tracy today."

She pushes her sleeves up and props her chin on her fists. "Busy day!"

"Yeah. I feel like shit about it too. I just dropped her like she was nothing."

"If you feel like shit, why are you smiling?"

He is appalled. It is true. "Why *am* I?"

"Because you're happy. You're in love. You like the new girl better than the old girl."

"But that's so callous. What about Tracy?"

"If Tracy comes in here for a session, I'll worry about Tracy. All I care about is, *you* are happy with your decision. So we move on. How are Mom and Josh?"

"All right." He can never think of anything to say about them. Then he suddenly has a question. He looks at Nancy pleadingly. "Why didn't I talk to Mom about Clarissa and Tracy? She asked me what happened today and I said nothing."

She grins. "How should I know? You tell me."

"It was almost like I didn't want her to know."

"Why?"

"Because . . . she might not understand."

"Is she dumb or something?"

"No! She's one of the most intelligent people I've ever known!"

"Well, your information isn't that complicated. Why do you think she wouldn't understand?"

"She might think. . . . I don't know."

"Yes, you do."

"I guess I mean I don't think she understands *me* all that well." He feels disloyal saying this. He hangs his head.

"Why not?"

"Because I'm so damned hard to understand!" he explodes. "That's why I'm here, right? She's a normal, well-balanced person, just like Josh. Neither of them— I'm just different from them. I'm a mess."

"In what way?"

"In every way. I'm all screwed up, aren't I? Just the fact that I come here . . ."

Once in a while Nancy gets very serious. Her eyes are neither hard nor playful, just kind. "Zachary, calm down a second. Let's get one thing straight. You're not screwed up. You're just here for nightmares. Outside of that, you're perfectly well adjusted. Just being in therapy—"

"All right, I know that. But Mom . . ."

"Mom what?"

"Well, she. . . . Everything is easy for her. She thinks I'm silly for coming here. When I first started having these dreams, she said I should watch what I ate before bed. That's how her mind works."

"Must be nice."

He sighs. "Yeah. I admire her."

"Well, something made you come here in spite of that. You knew it was more serious than she thought it was."

He sighs again. "Yeah."

"Zack. There's a fine line between contented and numb. Anybody who seems completely happy all the time is denying their emotions. I don't know if you should admire your mother or not. It sounds like she copes by just trivializing things. That's okay sometimes, but not if there's a serious problem."

"You don't understand," he says.

Nancy looks at him a long time, making some kind of assessment. He can tell there's something else she wants to say, but she holds it back. "We're making progress, Zack. At first your dreams were vague and so terrifying, it paralyzed you to talk about them. Remember?"

His early dreams. Full of motion. Someone always rushing him down corridors and through alleyways. He felt like he had run as fast as he could or they would be caught and something unspeakable would happen to them. He would wake up, drenched in sweat, screaming his head off, his heart beating so fast, it hurt. "Yeah."

"Now the images are getting specific. The apple trees. The tiger. The man. Some part of your mind is trying to send you a message, Zack. We just have to decide what kind of a message it is."

"Why doesn't it just come out and tell me?"

"Because you're so scared. You're too scared to hear it. But from coming here, you're getting calmer, and as that happens, the message will clear up."

Zack shivers, proving her point.

•

Driving home, Zack feels wonderful. He loves to drive, especially at night. He loves his car, a sharp little black Toyota his mom gave him for his sixteenth birthday. It wasn't like her to buy something so flashy and extravagant, so he cherishes it even more. He speeds a little, something he feels guilty about, but he's so free tonight, unburdened and absolved for another week. Through the moon roof the sky is black and the constellations are brittle and bright. The highway in front of him is infinite, like yards of silver satin.

•

When he gets home, Mom and Josh have already gone to bed. They both like to go to bed and get up early, the opposite of Zack. Just another way he's out of sync. Mom's room is dark, but there's a friendly, warm bar of light under the door of his and Josh's room.

Zack opens the door. Josh is sitting up in bed, looking like a kid in his plaid bathrobe, holding the dog with one arm and reading—Zack cracks up—*Lady Chatterley's Lover*. Beamer runs to Zack, thumping his legs with his tail while Josh blushes and gets defensive.

"It's for *school*."

"Sure it is. Are you getting the important parts? Like how the Industrial Revolution spoiled the natural beauty of England?"

Josh frowns. "Is that in there?"

Zack laughs, stripping in front of the mirror. He and Josh sleep in underwear, like soldiers. Zack is bigger and better built than Josh. He smiles at his reflection. Clarissa Benedetto will be impressed when she sees all this. "I'll give you some friendly advice," Zack says, combing his hair so he can enjoy his reflection a little longer. "That's a trick book. English teachers use it to trick you. They know you're just going to read the jerk-off parts and they nail you on all the other issues. Just remember what I told you. No matter what you think this book is about, it's about the Industrial Revolution. Got it?"

"Got it." Josh smiles, looking with open envy at his brother's body. "Do you think . . . girls really feel like it says in here? Like they have hot feathers inside them?"

"I don't know, I'll ask around." Zack puts the comb down and goes to his bed, followed closely by the dog.

Josh looks like he wants to ask more questions. He probably thinks Zack has done it, but he hasn't. Not quite. He and Tracy went pretty far, but she never quite let him do the deed. He wonders if he would lie about that.

But Josh is too shy to ask, thankfully. "You're in a good mood tonight," he says. "Did you have a good session?"

"Yeah. I had a lot to tell her. I met a new girl today."

"Really? Can I have Tracy?" Josh is serious too. Whenever Tracy was around the house, he went into an alpha state. Zack figures the masochist in Josh sensed the latent sadist in Tracy.

"Take your best shot. I dumped her today." Zack can hardly resist showing off in front of Josh because Josh encourages it.

"You did? Seriously?"

"Sure. Next to Clarissa, Tracy's dog food. Clarissa is—"

"You just met her today and you broke up with Tracy right away?"

"You'll understand when you're older. Clarissa is special. As soon as I met her Tracy bored me."

"What's she like?"

Pleasurably Zach invokes her memory. "Curly, curvy, dark, luminous, earthy, verdant, lush, fecund . . ."

Josh giggles. "You're making me hot and I don't even know half those words."

"She's an artist too. We're soul mates. It's destiny. She smells like lilacs."

"You better stop. I'll have to take a cold shower."

"It's that book. You shouldn't read that before you go to bed. You might have an accident."

"Shut up!" Josh giggles. But he loves it, loves having an older brother he can joke with about sex. His love for Zach shines in his eyes.

It makes Zach feel a little guilty. He loves Josh but not *that* much. Sometimes he thinks how nice only children have it. Still, it would be awful to go through something as scary as childhood all by yourself. "Joshua?" he asks suddenly.

"What?"

"Do you remember anything bad happening when we were kids?"

"Bad? Like what?"

"I don't know. Something really awful, maybe. Scary."

"Sure. That time you talked me into climbing out on the roof, and when Mom got ahold of us, she spanked the daylights out of us! That was very scary!"

"No, I mean worse than that."

"You don't remember how hard she spanked us!"

"Josh, I'm being serious now. Because Nancy says maybe my dreams are coming from some kind of bad memory from when I was little. I dreamed about a tiger. . . . Does that mean anything to you? Do you remember us going to the zoo or the circus or something?"

Josh's dark blue eyes are blank. "No. Honestly. I don't think it could be that. I mean apart from Dad dying, we had such a nice, normal childhood. Compared to other kids I talk to. It was tame city. We did go to the Cincinnati Zoo one time, remember? But nothing happened. The tigers were so far away, we could hardly see them. All I remember is eating Sno-Kones and riding that little train."

Zack sighs. "Yeah. You're right."

"I don't think dreams mean anything," Josh says. "I think you're just making it into a problem by dwelling on it."

"You sound like Mom."

"I think she's right. There's nothing wrong with you. You're one of the most together people I know. But if you start going to shrinks and poking around in your head, before you know it you will think you're screwed up."

"Yeah, maybe."

"You just worry too much. You always did."

"Yeah." Zack turns off his light. "Good night, Squirt."

Josh turns off his light. "Good night."

Zack pulls the dog in close and uses his shoulder for a pillow. By matching his breathing with Sunbeam's, he manages to fall asleep. Tonight the dream is not so bad. He's with Clarissa and they're lying in the grass beside a huge hedge of lilacs, kissing. It's spring and everything smells like rain. When the wind blows, lilacs shower down on them. Zack tries to enjoy himself, but he can't quite do it because he knows there's something on the other side of the hedge, crouching and waiting.

THREE

The final art assignment is always good. Zack has had four years with Mr. Taylor, and he knows the final assignment is always the pièce de résistance. The work that results will be exhibited in the halls for the Spring Art Show. Mr. Taylor has a genius for giving assignments. Last year he asked for a piece that expressed the passage of time. Philistines painted watches and clocks or made collages of their own baby pictures. Zack ran a piece of masking tape along the wall of the art room, out into the hall, down the stairs, and into the schoolyard with the words of Poe's sonnet "Silence" strategically placed. Students had to follow the tape, move through space and time, and end up in the yard feeling creepy. It was great.

Everyone knows today is the day. Zack is doubly excited because Clarissa Benedetto, all in black with a silver belt, is just a few feet away, paging through her science book, each flip of the page sending a gust of lilac wind to Zack's heart. Today he will ask her to lunch and persuade her to fall in love with him.

The bell rings. Mr. Taylor makes his majestic entrance, waving a book for effect. He comes to the center of the room and holds the book still for everyone to see. It is *The Picture of Dorian Gray*.

"This is a wonderful book about painters and painting," he says. With no other introduction, he opens the book and begins to read: ". . . *every portrait that is painted with feeling is a portrait of the artist—not of the sitter. The sitter is merely the accident, the occasion. It is not he who is revealed by the painter; it is rather the painter who, on the coloured canvas, reveals himself. The reason I will not exhibit this picture is that I am afraid that I have shown in it the secret of my own soul.*"

He puts the book down, pauses for effect. "I find that passage chilling. Every artist's greatest fear is that he will expose too much of himself, tell something he really doesn't want others to know. I think maybe this is where genius lies. To walk a fine line between revealing and concealing yourself. To expose everything inside you and yet disguise it so the audience isn't quite sure it's you." He pauses again. "Your final assignment is to make a piece in which you show the secret of your own soul. A piece that's about the part of you you keep hidden. The challenge for you is to tell your secret without letting us guess it. For that you will have to be very creative. Any questions?"

Kenny Leverson shoots up his hand. He always has a question or else he just likes the sound of his own voice. "I don't see how we can do this. If I paint some family secret or something, I'll get killed."

"I don't want your family secrets; I want *your* secrets,"

Mr. Taylor says patiently. "I want you to visualize the one thing you have always kept to yourself, that you wouldn't tell anyone, and put it into a piece. But naturally you won't want to expose yourself, so you will have to find some way of telling without telling. That's your challenge, and since you have a personal stake, you'll have to succeed. I think once you give thought to the assignment, you'll have no trouble. Anything else?"

Zack tunes out. He has no trouble. His choice is clear. He will paint a scene from one of his dreams. It's perfect. Obviously they represent his darkest secret, but the messages are so weird and coded, even he doesn't understand. He thinks maybe he will focus on the tiger. The tiger of his dreams is such a beautiful, magnificent animal. He would like to paint the shadowy man, but that image is unclear. The tiger will be perfect. Satisfied, he turns his attention to Clarissa. She is in a dream world, probably also thinking about her assignment. What is her darkest secret? Zack wonders. Probably her agonizing lust for him. That would look good on canvas.

Mr. Taylor is finished answering dumb questions. He tells them to use the rest of the period to plan the assignment and make sketches. Now is the moment of truth. Zack gets up and sits down next to Clarissa. She smiles at him.

"Do you like the assignment?" he asks her.

She laughs. "No, not really."

"Why? I think it's a great idea."

She opens her sketch pad. "I'm not crazy about telling my secrets to the whole world."

"But that's just the point! You're supposed to tell without telling! That's what makes it such a good assignment. I think Mr. Taylor's a genius."

Clarissa is sketching, angling the pad so he can't see. "He doesn't have to do the assignment."

Zack decides to change the subject. "You doing anything for lunch?"

She laughs again. "Yes, I'm joining some friends on a yacht. How about you?"

He doesn't know how to take her. She keeps him off balance. Still, he likes it. "I hate the cafeteria," he says. "I like to get out in the sunshine and eat."

"That sounds nice," she says.

"Want to come with me?"

She smiles a little. "I didn't bring any lunch."

"You can have half of mine."

"Won't you get hungry if you do that?"

"I'll survive. It . . . would be worth it to eat lunch with you." He waits, tense all over. He's out on a limb now. She could hurt him.

She stops sketching. Her eyes cruise back and forth, studying his face. "Sounds good to me."

•

It is a dazzling, sparkling spring day, the air noisy with blackbird whistles. He leads her to his favorite tree, a tall evergreen that paves the ground with soft, scented nee-

28

dles. She walks, not beside him but behind him, single file. Is she checking him out? No, girls don't think that way. Surely not. Zack prays to all the gods she doesn't hate peanut butter.

"Here," he says when they get to the tree.

They sit down cross-legged. He feasts on her beauty in the sun. A sloe-eyed beatnik in her black T-shirt and jeans. Her belt flashes like a horizontal river. Strange, reddish lights appear in her dark hair.

He reverently unzips his backpack. "Do you like peanut butter?"

"Love it," she says.

It's settled. He will marry her.

Neither of them talk while they eat. He likes that about her. She knows that out in nature you should shut up and listen. He used to wander off from Mom and Josh when they went to the beach because they would chatter about trivial crap and drown out everything the ocean was trying to say.

They share his peanut butter sandwich, his red grapes, his Symphony bar. She sips at his apple juice, sharing the same straw.

"I broke up with my girlfriend yesterday," he says casually.

"Really?" Her lovely eyes are still neutral. He can't read her at all.

"Yeah. It just didn't feel right. You know?"

"I do. I went with this guy back in New Jersey. We were

together almost a year. I think he thought it was . . . serious. He . . ." She trails off, looking into space.

"What was wrong with him?" Zack asks, looking for clues.

"He was boring."

Good. Good. Zack is pretty sure he isn't boring. Weird and psychotic, maybe, but not boring. "Tracy was kind of dull too," he says. "No surprises."

She smiles to herself as if she were thinking Zack won't have that problem with *her*.

"Do you miss up North?" he asks.

"No."

"Really? I left Ohio when I was five. I still miss it. Don't you think you'll miss the winters and the snow and—"

"I don't think that way," she says.

"Think what way?"

"Worry about losing things. I'm in Florida now, so I'll find out what I like about Florida. Once I'm done with something, I don't cry over it."

He is impressed but a little scared. She seems even more cold-blooded than he is.

She is looking at him funny now. A little slyly perhaps. Her eyes are warm, like coffee. "You're interested in me, aren't you?" she asks.

He chokes. "Interested?"

She laughs. "Do you want to go out with me?"

He feels a surge of arousal. No girl ever pursued him before. He likes it. "Yes, I do," he says quietly.

"Good. Because I really like you, Zack. I liked you from the first minute I saw you."

"Me too. I mean, you."

"I'm busy this weekend. Next Saturday?"

"Okay. . . . In the daytime. Let's go to the park or the beach or something. I like to be outdoors." This is true, but he's also scared of what she would do to him in the night. He feels out of control around her.

"Okay," she says. She finishes the apple juice and smiles at him. "Do you want to start calling me Clara?"

If he were alone, he would weep for joy.

•

First he is moving horizontally across plowed fields. No, they are rows of trees, acres and acres of apple trees, and as he moves he looks down the vast corridors between the rows of trees, a series of alleys that seem to go on for miles, plunging into the blue horizon. His eyes are almost stung by the flickering contrast, the trees so close, the horizon so far, the two things alternating so quickly it puts him in a trance.

Then he is standing still, looking down the long alleyway. Apple trees tower on both sides of him, two endless rows of trees, like walls. He feels his vision is unnaturally clear, he is seeing for hundreds of miles perhaps, with every detail in sharp relief. He thinks in his dream, How could there be an orchard so vast?

Then he sees the Man, a shadow, standing at the end of the row. It is the shadow of a man standing upright instead of lying on the ground as it should. Its arms are stretched out to Zack, pleading with him, calling him. Zack is happy, overjoyed. He runs into the corridor of trees.

Then he begins to see them, on both sides in his peripheral vision. Flashes of color. The wrong color. It should be masses of red and green. But he sees orange and black.

Zack freezes on the spot. He looks fearfully into the nearest tree. Sitting on the branches is a tiger, looking at him calmly. His tail curves down like a vine. He yawns and displays ferocious teeth.

Zack looks at another tree and another. Every tree has a tiger in its branches. The orchard is full of tigers, and if he makes a wrong move, they will spring on him and tear him apart.

He looks down the corridor, to the horizon. The shadow man is still there, still waiting. Zack wants to go to him. The Man is waiting, expecting him.

Slowly, trying not to look directly at the trees, Zack tries to creep along. Maybe if he stays calm, they won't bother him. At the edge of his vision he sees them, though, shifting their positions, turning to look as he passes, switching their tails, and flexing their huge paws.

His steps get slower and slower. He feels despair. It's too far to go forward and too far to go back. He's trapped now, the odds are against him. His fear seems to affect them. They are more restless now, prowling the branches and making rumbling sounds.

He looks in desperation to the Man, but the Man is gone. The horizon is empty. Zack feels ripped apart by grief and loneliness. He doesn't even care about his safety anymore. He sits on the ground and begins to cry.

All around him the tigers begin to climb down from the trees. They move toward him slowly and gracefully, a huge herd of them. They mill around him, sniffing at him and nudging him with their bodies. Some of them step on him with their huge, clumsy feet. He feels that somehow they will suffocate him with their fur. One tiger passes very close to his face and Zack pushes at him. The tiger whirls into a fighting stance, head low, eyes flashing gold fire. It emits a growl like thunder, and Zack knows he is going to die.

•

"Hey! Hey! Hey! Snap out of it." Joshua's voice comes to the rescue again, pulling him away from the tiger orchard.

"Josh?" Zack flails, finds an arm in the darkness and clings for dear life. Slowly the room assembles itself. The pale green glow of the night-light. The window. Josh. Safety.

"You okay?" Joshua peers at him.

"Now I am. I'm sorry. Did I scream?"

"No." A musical laugh. "But you were sort of *growling*. And you pushed the dog out of bed!"

That's how it looked to a normal person. Josh's world

was easy and fun. He had no idea that a moment ago the room had been full of tigers.

"I'm okay now," Zack says softly. "Go back to sleep."

"G'night!" Josh calls cheerfully.

Good night, you lucky shit, Zack thinks. He gets the dream diary out, turns on his flashlight, and dutifully writes his account. Then, because he is afraid to sleep again, he slides a sketch pad from under the bed and works for hours, trying to re-create what he has witnessed.

FOUR

Music. Sacred music. So much better than art because it's cleaner. More mental. It never makes a mess. Zack runs his finger down the program, marking off each piece as it's played. He has done this all his life, run his finger down the margins of countless programs at countless concerts and recitals. Always waiting for it to be over.

Now they are coming to the end and he can already feel relief, like a drug flooding into his bloodstream. He has made it through one more concert without screaming.

But the worst is still ahead. Josh's solo is naturally the grand finale, since he's the Greatest Musician to Ever Walk the Earth.

Zack fights the urge to go to sleep. It reminds him of being a little kid in church. All during the sermons Zack used to struggle and struggle not to give in and lose consciousness.

He knows how to wake himself up, though. He has merely to look to his left where his mother is sitting and see the beatific expression he knows is on her face. She never looks that way at an art show. But that's not fair. She's a musician herself. She understands what Josh has accomplished. She doesn't know enough about painting to appreciate Zack's work. It doesn't mean she loves him less.

He decides to look over. There she is with tears in her deep blue eyes. She wears her favorite dress for Josh's recital, a gorgeous forget-me-not blue. What will she wear two weeks from now at the Spring Art Show? Zack knows he will notice and then hate himself for noticing. But why does she have to look like that, like she's being transported or something? Can't she tone it down a little?

Applause startles him. They're down to the last piece, thank God. Josh's solo. Zack runs his finger down the program, keeping his eyes on the stage. Joshua comes shyly from the wings, keeping his head down as if the applause is something he's afraid will splash in his face. He looks good. Zack helped him pick the tie. It's a mauve paisley. Josh is so beautiful and virginal, blushing and ducking his head. The whole audience wants to kiss him. He sits down, sort of squirming on the piano bench, and looks to Mr. Grace, the music teacher, with eyes full of childish love. Mr. Grace smiles back and gives the cue.

Zack hates the piece after three notes. It is a thick, sticky sad melody, amberish in color, falling or slipping downward like honey dripping. Or like the sap running out of a tree. Zack consults the program. "Feuilles Mortes." He is listening to a song about dead leaves. Zack closes his eyes, trying to fight off depression. The music gives him no help. He looks at his mother.

It is worse than he expected. Her eyes are half closed as

if in a trance. He can see her adoration for Josh like a mist around her. She's turning into a brilliant blue fog, disintegrating right before his eyes. How can Nancy tell him with a straight face he's not screwed up? These can't be normal thoughts.

Zack tries to have a normal thought. *How wonderful to hear my talented brother play this dead-leaf music!*

Zack looks down at his hands and sees he has crushed the program in his fist.

•

"I don't want to hate my brother!" he wails to Nancy, who is—this must be a trick—filing her nails.

"I don't think you do," she says. "You always speak fondly of him to me."

"But during that concert I got so damned angry!"

"At what?" She pretends to concentrate on a tricky corner.

"Well, at Maurice Ravel for writing a song about dead leaves in the first place, and at my mom for having an orgasm listening to it—"

"Hold it." She actually extends her hand. "There you have it. Sibling rivalry. Case dismissed."

"Isn't that bad? Isn't that something I should work on?"

"Well, you can try, but the only people I know who don't suffer from it are only children. I have those feelings for my two sisters and I'm perfectly normal." She crosses her eyes to make him laugh.

"Do you think my mom loves him more?"

Nancy shrugs, puts her emery board away. "I'm a therapist, not a psychic. Besides, what difference does it make? It sounds like she loves you a lot. She never openly favors your brother, does she?"

"No, but . . ."

"Then let her off the hook. She loves you both. She's doing the best she can."

"No, but I feel like . . . I ought to do better. She doesn't love me as much as she could because I've done something wrong."

Nancy sits up straight. He knows from experience that means she's on to something. "Like what?"

"I don't know. It's just a feeling. I'm such an outsider in my family. They both play the piano and I'm a painter. They have brown hair and I have blond."

"Enormous obstacles." She laughs.

"I don't belong there!" he says.

She laughs again. "If you don't belong there, where do you belong?"

"I don't know!" he wails.

"Okay, okay. Let's change the subject. You're getting too upset to do yourself any good. Let's talk about life in general. How's Clarissa?"

"Clara. She's letting me call her Clara now."

"I told you she was an operator. Are you going out?"

"Our first date is Saturday. We're going to the park to draw."

"Sounds good. You like her a lot?"

"I think so. She scares me a little bit, but it's okay."

"My husband has the same effect on me. So it could be true love."

"I hope so. I'd like to have something go right for me."

"You have a lot going for you. Any new dreams?"

He reads to her from his diary, about the tiger orchard dream.

"Wow," she says when he's finished.

"Yeah. I think I'm going to paint it for my art class."

"I'd like to see that painting. Those tigers. I can't get a handle on how you feel about them. In the dream they seem to like you, but you feel suffocated by them."

"Yeah."

"But you like the man. You want to go to the man."

"Yeah. I want to run to him."

"Did you ever think you might be dreaming about your father?"

"Yeah. Maybe. But I never knew him."

"How old were you when he died?"

"Five."

"And you have no memories of him at all?"

"Nope. Mom said it was sort of a blessing that he died when Josh and I were so little. She says you can't miss what you never had."

"I don't know if I agree with that."

"Well, but it's true. I don't know what a father would feel like."

"But maybe you want to. Hence the dream. Here's this

male shadow reaching out to you. What did he die of? Was it sudden?"

"I'm not sure. I think so."

"Do you remember your mother grieving?"

"No. She didn't do that in front of us. She . . . keeps her emotions in. But I don't think she ever got over him."

"Why do you say that?"

"She can't stand to talk about it, even now. I guess you never get over a thing like that."

"What was he like? What do you know about him?"

"Well . . . not much. Just his name. Anthony Lloyd."

"What did he do for a living?" She is leaning forward like the needle on a compass.

"I don't know."

"What did he look like?"

"I don't know."

"You don't know!" She is almost shouting at him. "Haven't you ever seen a picture of your own father?"

"No!" He feels defensive. "I don't think there are any. I think when he died, Mom destroyed all the pictures of him. Like I said, she took it really hard."

"What about his parents? Your other grandparents. Where are they?"

"I guess I . . . don't know. I never thought about it."

"You never wondered about these things at all?"

"No! I mean, I never thought about it. Maybe they're dead or something. It never came up."

"When you were little, weren't you curious about your father? Didn't you try to ask questions?"

"I guess I did. But I could see . . . it was too painful for her. I didn't want to hurt her."

"But you have a right to know about your own father, don't you?"

"Well, sure, but . . . I don't know. Why is it important? If he's dead anyway."

"Because he's a part of you. Zack, this could be the whole basis of your nightmares. If you've repressed all your natural curiosity about your father, of course it's going to try and come out in some weird way."

"I don't think I feel any curiosity about him. He's dead. Finding out things about him won't bring him back."

Nancy looks at him a long time. Then she looks at her watch. "Your time was up five minutes ago."

He feels rejected. Or worse, punished. She is punishing him for not agreeing with her. He stands up on shaky legs and walks out of her office with his head down.

•

Driving home, he presses the gas pedal teasingly, watching the needle creep past the posted speed limit, then past his usual speeding speed. Tonight he wants to be bad. He wants to push it to the limit. The highway is like molten silver beneath his wheels. The wind whips his face, stripping away all his fears and worries. He is free. He is on the verge of some kind of dramatic escape.

The other cars on the interstate become toys, obstacles to navigate. He tailgates, passes, cuts off. People honk at him. He feels deliciously wicked, like some other person. Some colorful outlaw.

The other cars become little flashes as he whips past them. Silver. Blue. Flame. Black. Black again. Blue and white. . . . Oh, God. Blue and white. Zack has just whipped past a police cruiser at—he consults the speedometer—eighty-five miles per hour.

Sweat breaks out everywhere. His foot becomes weak and impotent. The needle wavers and drops. His face is hot, embarrassed. He's going to get it. He just knows he's going to get it. All he can think of is his mother. What will she do if he gets a speeding ticket? What will she think of him?

He looks in his rearview. The cruiser has pulled into his lane, right behind him. He can see the cop looking at him in the mirror, smiling a little, sadistic. He doesn't turn on his siren or his lights. He's just going to follow Zack awhile and watch him suffer.

Zack is breathing hard now, shaking. There's a horrible squirmy feeling in his stomach that spreads down into his genitals. He remembers that feeling. It happened in the third grade. He was in the rest room and some fifth grade boys were smoking. Just after they put out the cigarettes, a teacher came in. He wanted to know who was doing it. No one, including Zack, would say a word. So everyone had to go to the principal's office.

Zack had never been to the principal's office. He hardly even knew the man. Mr. Foster. He had a white mustache and cold eyes. He told Zack he was an accessory to the crime unless he would tell which boys were smoking. Zack wouldn't do it. He thought it would be wrong to tell. Mr. Foster said if that was his attitude he was guilty, too, and he'd have to take a paddling.

Zack, who never got in any kind of trouble, was terrified. All he could think of was his mom. She would think he was some kind of bad kid. She didn't want the kind of son who was punished in the principal's office. Still, he just couldn't squeal on another kid. So he had to stand up and bend over, putting his hands on the seat of a chair. And he had to wait in that position while Mr. Foster called in his secretary as a witness and got the paddle down off the wall. And still he made Zack wait a little for the first swat. That was the terrible part. That was the part that nearly killed him. Having to stay in that humiliating posture, meekly offering his backside to that stranger. He was angry. He knew his face was red, and he felt that squirming, gripping feeling down in the roots of him. He knew Mr. Foster could see him trembling, and he knew Mr. Foster was enjoying that. He was making him wait on purpose, laughing at him.

Just like this cop. He is smelling Zack's fear like a shark smelling blood, and he is going to follow Zack for miles and miles now, laughing at him, making him suffer.

Zack tries to fight it. There is nothing to be afraid of now, he tells himself. He's been going fifty-three for ten minutes. That cop wouldn't dare pull him over now. But the feeling in Zack's body is too strong. He isn't eighteen anymore. He's a little third grader, and that cop is going to pull him over and haul him out of the car and paddle his ass in front of everybody on Interstate 95.

Zack is sweating so much, he can hardly hold the steering wheel. Why are people so cruel? What is that cop getting out of this nasty game? Zack is almost blind with rage, but he knows there's nothing he can do.

Maybe he can exit. Maybe the cop won't follow him on surface streets. It will take longer to get home, but he's got to get away from this unbearable tension. He pulls into the exit lane. The cop flies on past. But Zack sees his face. The bastard is openly laughing. He won some kind of contest against Zack and it makes him feel good.

He takes his time driving home, meandering along the surface streets. His body is soaked in sweat and he is still shaking. He has to get calm before he walks in the door or his mother will guess that something happened. It would be awful if she found out he was speeding and driving recklessly. She'd think he was some kind of horrible person.

That's the thing. He just can't let her know what he's really like. How bad he really is. She won't understand. She never found out about that paddling. He forged her name on the note. If she thought she had the kind of son who got paddled in school, he wouldn't have a chance.

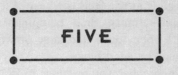

FIVE

Zack has never known anyone with curly hair before. Walking from his car, with their sketch pads, he watches with fascination how the wind lifts one curl at a time, gently tossing and rearranging. Could an artist capture that? It would be worth a try.

Zack is practicing abdominal breathing exercises because he is on his first date with the most exciting girl he's ever known and it just has to work. If anything goes wrong this afternoon, he knows he will die.

He has selected Tradewinds Park. Mullins Park is closer to home, but the name isn't romantic enough for Zack. And there is a little pontoon dock at Tradewinds Park he likes. He leads her there now.

Today Clara wears blue; work shirt, jeans, and thick white socks with high-tops. But she can't resist a little adornment, so she has unbuttoned the top two shirt buttons and hung a gold filigree cross around her neck. It swings in and out of her shirt in a maddening way, flashing in the sunlight one moment and dropping into the mysterious shadows the next.

He shyly shows her the dock as if it were something he built himself. She accepts it and he is thrilled. They walk out, Clara giggling as she feels the sway of it. They sit on the planks and arrange their equipment. Both have backpacks with their lunch and large drawing portfolios that buck when the wind blows.

"Do you know what you're going to do?" Clara asks him, squinting at a pencil.

For a moment he is horribly confused. He had been planning his romantic strategy. Now he realizes she is asking about his art project. "Yes," he says, struggling not to blush. "But I don't know if I want to tell you about it."

She opens her portfolio and studies a blank page. "I'm not going to tell you what my painting means," she assures him. "But I'll tell you what I'm going to paint. I'm going to paint the George Washington Bridge."

"Where's that?" Zack asks, feeling stupid.

She confirms this, glancing up with disapproval. "It crosses the Hudson River. It connects New York and New Jersey. It's a famous bridge."

"I didn't know." He hangs his head. She will never love him. Luckily curiosity diverts him. He looks up. "You're going to draw a bridge in New Jersey from memory? Without a picture in front of you?"

"Sure." She is making preliminary strokes, dividing her space horizontally and vertically.

"I don't think I'd trust myself to remember that well," he says.

She looks up. "I've looked at this bridge a lot. What are you going to draw?"

"Well . . ." he says. "A tiger orchard."

"A what?" She looks delighted.

"An orchard full of tigers." He smiles. He's pleased her. He's atoned for not knowing his geography.

She has even stopped drawing. "What does that mean?"

He grins. "We weren't supposed to tell."

She leans forward. The cross reappears. "Oh, pretty please?"

Zack wages a brief struggle with his nether regions. "I'll tell if you'll tell," he says.

Her coyness falls away. "No. Never mind." She looks down at her pad again.

He can't work at first because he wants to watch her work. She gives off a wonderful feeling of . . . containment. She is so serene. She's only been in this park five minutes and already she is in harmony with the surroundings. Now that she is looking down, Zack can appreciate the thickness and length of her eyelashes. Everything about her is still, under control. Only two points of motion. The measured stroke of the pencil and the wind-tossed curls. Zack, who is uneasy most of the time, feels a tremendous peace. He leans back against the wooden rails, for once in his life not checking for spiders or ants. He broadens his gaze to include the woods behind her. There is some kind of strange counterpoint between Clara and the woods. What is it? Then he realizes. The wind is swirling the leaves the same way it swirls her hair.

She looks up. "You aren't working."

He is too mellow for inhibitions. "I was looking at *you*."

She smiles. "No fair. I'd rather look at you than draw too. But we should get our work done first."

First? First? Before what? What is she going to let him do? Zack picks up his pencil with a trembling hand.

•

After a while he is lost in his work. Art is like sleep to Zack. He begins in a shallow state of concentration that slowly deepens into a trance. Subliminally he hears the birds and the wind, but he isn't really in the park anymore. He is somewhere in his own mind, trying to retrieve the feelings of that dream.

Although he has never used the style before, he knows this painting should be a mock-primitive. Everything will be flat and geometric, the colors unmixed and unnaturally flat. The tigers in the trees will be uniform, all in the same pose, all looking at the viewer with identical gaping eyes. Each tail curling down through the branches, like an inverted question mark.

The trees will be in perfect rows, as in the dream. He wonders if fruit trees really are planted this way. The rows will fan out toward the viewer and recede to a single point on the horizon, drawing the eye to the center of the canvas where the shadow will be standing. The tigers, as Zack works them out, become very much like the Cheshire cat—at once friendly and dangerous.

For hours he and Clara work in silence and everything flows for Zack, but there is always something in a composition that poses problems. Zack has never known it to fail. In this one the problem is the shadow man. It was a clear image in the dream, but Zack can't translate it to paper. How, for instance, can he convey the proper darkness and still keep it transparent? And he wants to capture the spirit of the dream, the way the shadow reached out to him; but if he tries to show that, the image becomes three-dimensional, and shadows exist in only two dimensions. It is maddening. Zack tries different tactics and begins erasing and drawing over the same spot. Soon everything is looking smudgy and wrong. It makes him furious. The rest of it, the apple trees and the tigers, is so easy and so perfect. Why is the shadow being so stubborn? He erases an arm angrily and tears a hole in the paper. "Damn!" he cries involuntarily.

Clara looks up with surprise. "What is it?"

He slams his portfolio shut. "It's all screwed up," he says. "Don't look at it. I hate it."

She gazes at him—he thinks, disapprovingly. "Don't be so hard on yourself." There is an edge in her voice that scares him.

For God's sake, don't blow this. Bad enough to ruin the drawing. But don't act like an ass and scare the girl off too. Zack feigns nonchalance. "I'm not," he says. "I just — Don't you get upset when you can't quite capture something?"

She keeps on looking at him, weighing. Scrutinizing. "I'll bet you're hungry," she says. "We've been working for hours."

"Oh, of course that's it!" he says desperately. "I'm always a jerk when I'm hungry or tired or anything like that. Let's eat."

Finally she gives him a smile. A little one. She puts her work away neatly and unzips her backpack. "I made a surprise for you," she says. "Do you like chocolate chip cookies?"

"Oh, yes, they're my favorite!" he says in a pleading tone.

"Well. Eat your sandwich like a good boy and maybe I'll give you one."

Zack eats his sandwich like a good boy. He knows he has just had a very narrow escape.

●

After lunch they take the de rigueur nature walk through the woods, following a plank walkway that keeps them safe from the dangerous things that prowl the Florida hammocks. Zack is not comfortable here, but Clara is a newcomer to Florida, and the smallest lizard, the tiniest wildflower, enchant her. Zack yearns for the safe woodlands of the Midwest, where the snakes, if there were any, were harmless and the shadows not quite so deep and twisted. He finds himself scanning the swampy terrain for northern things. He has raptures over a red maple sapling. He ignores a bittern and gazes at a mourning dove.

Deep in the woods Clara takes his hand. Just like that, as if they'd been lovers for years. Zack is instantly self-conscious. Is his hand too stiff? Too limp? Should he squeeze? And why didn't she let him make the first move?

He feels he's coming off as some kind of wimp, here. He was never this passive and confused with Tracy. But of course he didn't care about her.

Still, he feels he's got to assert himself a little. She stops to look at a fallen tree, and he puts his arms around her and pulls her into a kiss.

She responds as if she'd been waiting for it. Her kiss is warm and friendly. Zack can feel it all over. He gathers her closer, allows one hand to drift down her back, hesitate a second, then cup the rounded seat of her jeans. He wonders if she can feel his erection against her. She is so crushable and soft. He is dizzy from the scent of lilacs. She artfully inserts her tongue into the proceedings. No, no, that's too much. A man can only take so much standing up. He steps away, breathing hard. "Wow."

She giggles and looks brazenly at his crotch, proud of her handiwork. "We'd better watch our step!" she says happily.

He knows he's blushing. "Yeah," he says breathlessly.

"You want to walk some more?" she asks.

"In a minute," he says, and they both have to laugh at that.

Then suddenly her eyes get serious. "Zack. I really, really like you." She looks into his eyes.

He can still smell the lilacs. He wants to fall into that lovely trance again. He clears his throat and takes a deep breath. "Let's *walk*," he says urgently.

Her laughter echoes in the woods.

•

Later they stretch out on a shady hillside and finish Clara's cookies and draw some more. Zack finds a solution to his problem and works feverishly. When he finally looks up, Clara has put her work away and is sitting with her knees pulled up, staring at the western sky. The sun is low and the light is deep and gold. "What time is it?" Zack asks.

She consults her watch. "Five thirty. You really get lost in your work."

"This painting is going to be special," he explains. "It will be the best thing I've ever done."

She laughs, pleased. "How do you know?"

"I just know."

She reaches for the pad. "Let's see."

"Well . . . okay." He tips it in her direction.

"Oh!" She crawls over beside him for a better look. "How . . . weird. It's beautiful. What does it mean?"

Suddenly he wants to tell her. He wants to share everything about himself with her. "It's a dream I keep having. A recurring dream. About this shadow and these apple trees and tigers." He goes on to explain the specific plot. "I think it's some kind of memory from my childhood I'm trying to bring up." He decides to hold back on the fact that he's in therapy. At least for now.

"Wow. Did you ever have a little stuffed tiger? Or maybe a picture on your bedroom wall?"

"No," he says, thinking deeply. "But . . . I love the

sound of the word *tiger*. It makes me feel so good. I think if I ever did meditation, that would be my mantra. Tiger, tiger, tiger."

"Like the poem. 'Tiger, Tiger, burning bright.' "

"What's that?"

"Don't you know it? We just had it last semester. Blake . . . William Blake. It was a neat poem. I have it at home. I'll show it to you sometime."

"Okay."

"And you have no idea what your dream means?"

"No. I hope I'll understand it someday, though."

"That's really interesting," she says. "So the secret of your painting is even a secret to you?"

"That's right," he said. "Now show me yours."

She giggles. "I beg your pardon?"

"Your drawing!" He laughs.

She smiles coyly. "All right." She opens her portfolio and shows the sketch. It is not what he expected. He thought it would be a boat's eye view, but the point of view is from up on the bridge, looking through a mass of ironwork to the water below. On the shore the buildings are tiny, so the bridge appears to be miles and miles in the air. Between the bridge and the water a lone bird is soaring.

Zack shivers. "It looks scary."

"Good," she says. "That's the point."

"Is the bridge really this high?"

She looks at the drawing. "I guess I exaggerated for effect. That's the feeling I get on that bridge. That it's unearthly. It's like nothing moves when you stand up there. Even with all the traffic and the noise. It's like time stops and the world is so far away. . . . I threw a penny off that bridge once and it just kept falling and falling. I thought it was going to fall forever." It is the first time he has ever seen her like this, really vulnerable. She looks almost like a different girl.

"I guess you went to this bridge a lot," he says.

"I did for a while. Then I stopped."

He can feel there is a tremendous story here. "What does that bridge mean to you?" he says, stealing Nancy's line.

She looks up like someone waking. Then a kind of shield comes down, in her eyes. The lost look is gone. "Who knows what anything means to anybody?" she says.

He holds her eyes, determined. "You can tell me," he says. "I care about you."

She looks at him thoughtfully. Then she puts her arms around his neck and he's awash in the lilac tide again, feeling the undertow. This time it takes him down. He finds himself on his back, with her on top, kissing and kissing. Where did that girl learn these things?

There's no one around and he's too hot to care anyway. Her cross is swinging above him, catching the sunset and blinding him. He unbuttons her shirt. She is luscious, white lace cups loaded and straining. He touches gently with his fingertips as if reading braille; finds a mild hardening under the lace.

He rolls over to position himself on top of her, kissing cleavage. His denim rubs hard against her denim.

"Zack," she says softly. "No. We're out in public."

Oh, damn. She's right too. Who invented "out in public" anyway? No one should have to stop something this good just because it's publicly offensive and a crime. Still, he would hate to call home from his holding cell and explain to his mother he was caught being lewd in a park.

Reluctantly he lets the joyful feeling recede. He pulls away from her and sits in the grass, alone and throbbing, while she buttons and arranges herself. The sun has gone down.

"If it just wasn't a public park," she says, touching his shoulder lightly. "That's all."

He is still sick with disappointment, but he hears her. Some other time, some other place. . . . He turns to her. She is ten times lovelier now, all flushed and tousled. "You really get to me," he says.

She laughs, since this is already obvious. "It's mutual," she tells him. Then she leans forward and gives him a little kiss on the bridge of his nose. "We have to go. They expect me for dinner."

It is not until he has dropped her off and is driving home alone that he realizes what she did. She diverted him on purpose so she wouldn't have to answer his questions.

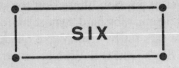

SIX

Mom and Josh are pretending it's spring. Zack and Beamer know better. In Florida there is no spring because there is no winter to recover from. The only change Zack has noticed is that the fire ants are biting more. Not something you want to dance around the maypole about.

He knows he should get himself in line. Lately Nancy has been hammering him about positioning himself as the outsider in the family. She says whatever you tell yourself over and over becomes reality. Zack doesn't believe it. If it were true, all the arrogant people in the world would be worth something.

And why shouldn't he feel like an outsider? Look at the two of them now, trimming the bougainvillaea with perfect coordination. Mom has the clippers, and Josh, the Mickey Mouse work gloves. He seems always to know exactly where she wants to clip, and is ready, holding the branch just as she aims for it. They seem to be functioning on a common brain, like hive insects. Zack knows if he went over to help, he'd grab the wrong branch. Zack hates the bougainvillaea anyway. A while ago, trying to get involved, he brought over a trash bag and picked up

56

some clippings. Instantly, a thorn stabbed him in the finger, just like Sleeping Beauty. His blood splashed disgracefully on the clean Chattahoochee. Mom and Josh had exchanged a glance: *Isn't he pitiful?*

Then Josh had taken the trash bag out of Zack's hand. "You have to handle them gently or they prick you," he said.

Prick you! Zack thought, sucking his finger and feeling like a toddler.

"Go in the house and wash that *thoroughly*," Mom had said.

Feeling rejected and dismissed, he dutifully went into the house and scrubbed the wound. When he came back out, they had resumed their comfortable rhythm, clipping and murmuring to each other. Someone had cleaned up his blood.

Now he is mowing the lawn. You don't need to be gentle for that, you just *shove*. It's a good activity for a bitter, angry person. Zack works up a sweat, not even sure why he is in a blind rage but giving it full vent. He leaves the bag off and shoots a tremendous arc of clippings in his wake, which Beamer plays tag with. Mom and Josh ignore him. It's as if he were just a boorish yardman they have to tolerate in their garden.

No. Come on, he tells himself. They aren't thinking those things, Nancy has pointed out. He, Zack, is doing it to himself. But why? If he wants to belong, why does he perpetuate this fantasy of being shut out? Last Thursday

Nancy had the nerve to suggest that it was Zack who was rejecting them! But why? For what? They are all he has.

Suddenly he feels awful, awful. These moods have come over him ever since he's been in therapy. A sweeping, defeated melancholy like a black hole, sucking in everything. He is so sad, his arms and legs weaken. He shuts off the mower and sits in the grass, hands covering his face. *Please, God, don't let me cry.*

Mom and Josh don't notice anyway. They're getting ready to plant some impatiens they bought at Wal-Mart this morning.

Beamer cares, though. He jumps at Zack's arms, breaking the barricade to lick his face. Zack embraces him shamelessly, clinging to his fur, pressing his cheek against the dog's strong shoulder, inhaling his scent. *Okay.* He's steady now. Zack stands up carefully and switches the mower back on. *Okay.* He begins to push, focusing on the green blur ahead, not daring to look toward the flower beds.

•

By the time the yard is finished, he feels good again. He looks at them now as they methodically turn the soil, and it's okay. He loves them. He will prove it. He goes into the house, strips to the waist, towels himself, and puts on a clean T-shirt. He wet-combs his hair. Beamer waits for him in the kitchen, pointing out discreetly that his Iams is getting low. Zack gives him a refill. Then he opens the refrigerator and takes out a big bottle of Evian water.

That's something all three of them have in common, a passion for Evian. It's the only beverage pure enough to meet their standards.

Getting tricky now, he frosts three glasses in the freezer compartment and arranges a tray. Mom has a little vase of hibiscus on the windowsill, and he adds that. More, more. He takes out a good china plate, fills it with Lemon Coolers. Beautiful. Is this the gesture of a loving son and brother or what?

"Wanna come?" he asks Beamer as he opens the back door with his foot.

Beamer is eating. There is no question of interrupting that for a human party. Balancing the tray carefully, Zack swings out the door.

The impatiens still aren't planted. Mom and Josh are squatting in the driveway, reading the instructions on a forty-pound bag of fertilizer.

"Maybe any blooming plant likes acid," Josh is speculating.

"I don't know," Mrs. Lloyd says. "Impatiens aren't listed here."

"Ta-da!" Zack interrupts, then braces himself for possible rejection.

"Oh, how lovely! The perfect thing!" says his mother, getting up to look at his tray. Josh seems a little reluctant to leave the fertilizer, but he finally does.

Mrs. Lloyd swiftly arranges the patio furniture to accommodate them. "You did a good job on the yard," she says to Zack.

He's living right. He sits down in a white wrought iron chair and picks up a cookie. "Thanks, Mom."

Josh can't get his mind off the fertilizer. "Zack, do you think if azaleas like acid soil then impatiens would too?"

"Sure," Zack says. "Anything that produces flowers. And evergreens like acid too." He got A's in biology.

"See, I told you," Josh says to Mom.

"Okay, I just wasn't sure."

Josh gives his brother a sly look. "Are you going to call Clara today?" he asks. Last night Zack had to give him a blow-by-blow description of his day in the park, and now Josh is overstimulated.

"You have to call her Clarissa," Zack says. "Only a few people can call her Clara."

"Oh! I beg your pardon!" Josh says, bowing.

"Who are we talking about?" Mrs. Lloyd asks. To a stranger her voice would sound bright and pleasant, but Zack hears an edge.

Josh doesn't. "Zack's new girlfriend. She's—" He seems to catch himself on the verge of saying something obscene. "—Italian."

Mrs. Lloyd looks at Zack. "Oh?"

Zack squirms. "She's a very nice girl, Mom. She just transferred. She's in my art class. We're both interested in art." Even he can hear how stupid this is. It's as if he were trying to convince her there's nothing *sexual* about it.

"What happened to Tracy?" she asks mildly. But Zack hears the true question: *Why am I not kept up-to-date?*

"I broke up with her."

"Oh." She takes a thoughtful sip of water. "Well, why don't you have her come over sometime? I'd like to meet her."

"Sure. I intend to. We just met. Yesterday was our first date."

"Well . . ." she says, looking down. She sets her glass aside.

Zack feels frantic. What has he done? It's all his fault, being so evasive and secretive. There is a wall between them, and it's his doing. But Nancy says it doesn't have to be that way. All he has to do is open up and his mother will open up too. He throws caution to the wind. "Mom?"

"Hmmm?" She looks up indifferently. Her eyes are so beautiful.

"There's something I really want to talk about. It's important to me."

The eyes soften. He must have sounded sincere. Even Josh looks up, interrupting his cookie binge. "It's about . . . Dad."

Josh puts down the cookie in his hand.

At first Mrs. Lloyd doesn't react. She just holds his gaze. "What about him?"

Zack blushes. He can feel the heat in his face. They are both staring at him as if he were doing something wildly inappropriate. He keeps his eyes on the grass. "Well, in therapy . . . it's kind of coming out that I don't know very much about him and that maybe that's part of my trouble, you know, with the dreams. That I feel some kind of need—"

"I see," she interrupts. "What is it you want to know?"

He feels like a heel. "If this is too painful for you . . ."

"No, no," she says. "If this is what your . . . *therapist* thinks you should do . . . what do you want to know?"

He looks up at her. Her face is bravely resolute. Josh is glaring at him. Everything seems unnaturally quiet. Zack speaks in a low tone. "Well, I mean, for instance, what did he die from? I realized I never knew."

"He had a bad heart."

"Oh." He shifts in his chair. "Okay. Well, what did he do for a living?"

She takes a deep breath. "He took a lot of odd jobs. Waited tables, did phone solicitation, that kind of thing. Most of the time he was unemployed."

This is a shock. Zack always imagined he was some kind of professional. A schoolteacher like Mom. Why would she have hooked up with such a loser? Maybe she had to. Maybe . . . No, let's take one trauma at a time. "What did he . . . look like?"

She squares her shoulders. "Actually . . . he looked a lot like you."

Despite the knifelike tension in his body, this comes through as a rush of joy. Zack looks like someone! A dead, worthless drifter with a bad heart, but at least *someone*. "Do we have a picture anywhere?" he begs in a whisper.

Her eyes drop. "No," she says quietly. "I got rid of them when . . . I suppose it was a foolish thing to do but—"

"That's enough, Mom," Josh says. "You don't have to say any more. Zack didn't mean to upset you."

"I know," she says softly.

"Let's get back to the flowers," Josh urges her.

She looks up. "All right." The two of them stand almost in unison and return to the little plot of ground they have prepared. In a moment they are making their little murmur again.

Zack feels like he's been slapped. He really hurt her and she'll never forgive him. He had to be cute and put himself in therapy and dredge up things to hurt her. What a self-indulgent bastard. No wonder she prefers her other son.

Tears burn his eyes. He stands up and clears the table. Neither of them looks at him. He dumps the whole tray, flowers and all, in the sink and runs hot water over it. Kill it.

Then he staggers into the living room and falls heavily on the couch beside the dog. The impact wakes Beamer up. He glances at Zack, stretches, jumps down, and walks out of the room. Of course, it is just a coincidence. Beamer isn't rejecting Zack. He's just going for a drink of water or something. But that is the final thing that makes Zack cry.

·

Later, after a phone call to Clara has calmed him, Zack feels the call of the highway. He makes polite excuses to the yard crew, who seem to have forgiven him. He even offers to bring home Chinese food. Then he heads for his beautiful black Toyota. Beamer comes along, thinking it's a normal trip in the car. He doesn't know his best friend is a closet thrill junkie. He hops right in and sits up straight in the passenger seat. Zack wonders if he would wear a seat belt. He buckles himself in, then pulls the shoulder harness across the dog's chest and locks it into place. Not a murmur of protest. But then, if you'd walk on a leash, why would you mind a seat belt? This makes Zack feel minimally better about taking his pal out for a bout of reckless operation.

Zack opens all the windows as soon as they are on the road. Beamer casually leans to his right. No big deal, just resting his back. The breeze teases his right ear. He looks coyly at Zack.

"Just watch it," Zack warns. But he will be lenient today. He knows how it feels when your parents don't understand you.

Coral Springs is a long way from the interstate. Zack gets restless, plodding along at thirty-five. He can taste the wind already, can picture that thrilling hypnotic blur of asphalt. Why does he love this so much?

Beamer puts one paw on the edge of the window.

"Uh-uh!" Zack says.

Beamer looks over as if bewildered.

"You know what I'm talking about!"

The paw is withdrawn.

Zack ruffles the top of Beamer's head. "Good boy. I'll let you have an egg roll later."

Finally the on ramp! "Hold on to your flea collar!" Zack calls as the roar of the wind drowns out the sound of his voice.

The risk of getting caught now, he knows, is even greater. When he speeds at night, he feels invisible; but in daylight a cop can spot him a hundred miles away. Also he can really see the faces of the other drivers as he whips around them. They hate him. They think he's some kind of bad kid. It's great. He laughs to himself.

Then he feels guilty. He shouldn't be laughing. It's really no joke how scared and exposed he feels, doing this blatantly wrong and dangerous thing in broad daylight, courting his worst fears. But he can't help it. The sucking roar of the wind is like a drug. He has never known such freedom.

The asphalt sparkles in the sun like a silver-black ocean. Joy rises in his chest and fills his throat. He looks over to see if Beamer is having a good time.

"Hey!" Zack yells.

Beamer must be a wind addict too. He has given up on being a good boy and earning an egg roll. He's leaning halfway out the passenger window, holding the seat belt away from his body. His ears and tongue flap in the breeze. The roar is so great out there, he doesn't even hear Zack's reprimand.

Zack eases up on the pedal, feeling guilty for driving like this and putting his best friend in danger. He leans over and taps Beamer's shoulder. "Hey," he says.

Beamer pulls in his head fast and goes into the full

submission act, whining softly as if he thought Zack might take a pop at him.

"It's okay," Zack says. "But don't do that. You could get hurt."

The game is no fun anymore. Zack is at fifty-five now, and he feels really weird. At first he thinks it is guilt for driving recklessly with Beamer. But it's not that; it's . . . almost a kind of nervous urgency at the back of his mind, like when you know you're supposed to do something but you can't remember what. It seems almost like—

A loud horn makes him jump. His heart pounds. He has swerved a few inches out of his lane, distracted by the funny feeling.

That's enough interstate driving for today, he thinks. He takes the next exit, Broward Boulevard, and heads into downtown Fort Lauderdale, feeling almost grateful for the posted speed limits and the proximity of the police station. Here he won't be tempted to sin.

But that feeling . . . what is it? It's still there. Something happened when he tapped the dog. It has happened before. It happened . . . with his *father.*

Zack shivers. It's true. He knows it like he knows his own name. He was riding somewhere in a car with his father. And he, Zack, put his head too far out the window, and his father tapped him just like that and said "Hey." He can hear his father's voice! It's tenorish, kind of soft. A nice voice.

Zack has to stop the car. He can't drive and deal with this. He pulls into the city parking garage and just sits there in a daze, wondering if this is real. He tries to concentrate on the image, to retrieve more information. If only he could see his father's face! Or his arm or anything. But mostly he remembers the view out the window, the asphalt running under the car like silver. That's what lured him out. And he has liked it ever since. And he remembers looking at himself in the passenger mirror. Seeing his little-kid face in a red, right-hand mirror. This is an image from one of his dreams! Nancy's right! These dreams are memories of his father! He can remember the mirror clearly. It had words printed on it. But Zack couldn't read at the time. "What does this say?" he had asked his father.

"Objects in the mirror are closer than they appear."

"What does that mean?"

"Well . . . like it says."

"Oh."

He has captured the whole moment. The whole exchange. And he can remember his feelings for his father. Warm and happy feelings. He loved his father! He never knew this before.

His mind is racing to make sense of this. He prays this is something real and not just wishful thinking. Nancy has warned him about telling a therapist what you think she wants to hear. But he just knows. He knows that was a real red car and a real conversation. He knows it in his bones and in his blood. Someday maybe all of it will make sense, even the tigers. The funny thing is, if his memory is so pleasant—and it is—why are his dreams like nightmares?

It doesn't matter, now that he has a secret treasure. Anthony Lloyd, he now knows, drove a red car with racing mirrors and spoke in a wonderful warm, soft voice. And that scrap of information has changed the whole world.

SEVEN

"This is really interesting, Zack. I mean it. But I just don't think we should open the champagne yet." Nancy is in black today, some kind of sleeveless thing with a zipper in front, like what you'd wear for bike racing or skin diving. She's not as flat-chested as Zack thought. He struggles with transference.

"It's real," he says. "I know it's real. I remember him. It's not a fantasy."

"You're not in a position to say." She rummages her purse, which looks like a black bowling bag. Zack hopes she is out of cigarettes. "You'd be surprised what the subconscious will conjure up just because you request it. Dreams are all about that. Your conscious mind is mad at somebody. Bang! You have a dream that they're dead. It aims to please. Right now your subconscious has heard both of us saying that maybe you have repressed memories of your father. Presto! It builds you a little fantasy. Daddy's driving you in the car, watching out for you, just like you're taking care of your dog. See? I mean you need this. It's a powerful need, especially at your age. Think about the symbolism. Red sports car? Dual racing mirrors? Is that a phallic symbol or what?" She snickers.

"It's not!" Zack says, really angry. "I know the difference between fantasizing and remembering. I do both! If it was a phallic symbol, why didn't I pick a town car or something? This was like a little Pinto!"

She laughs hard. "Maybe you have modest aspirations!"

Usually he likes her jokes, but not today. "Why don't you believe me?" he wails. "I'm telling you. I remembered him. I heard his voice. It was a real voice. I know it!"

She can't find her cigarettes, puts her purse aside. "Calm down. I'm not calling you a liar. I just don't want you to get your hopes up for no reason. There's about a fifty-fifty chance this is a genuine memory. That's my professional opinion. If it is genuine, you'll probably have more. And now that you've remembered him, your nightmares should stop. That would be the acid test."

Zack lowers his head. He considers for the first time the possibility of lying to her.

"Have you had any nightmares since the 'memory' came to you?" she asks.

He can't lie to her. He plays with his fingers. "Yes."

"When?"

"Last night."

"Did you put it in your diary?"

"Not yet."

"Tell me about it."

He keeps his head down. "Mom's taking me to the zoo. I'm a little boy. Josh isn't there. We come to a cage where there's a big, gorgeous tiger and he likes me, so I reach through the bars and pet him. And it's great, he just purrs like a little kitten. But Mom gets really mad at me and says, 'Leave him alone, he's dangerous.' But I don't want to. I say, 'Just one more minute?' and she gets really mad. I mean furious. Scary. And she opens the cage and lets the tiger out and she puts me in the cage and goes off and leaves me there."

Nancy is silent. Finally he looks up. She is gazing at him sympathetically. He realizes for the first time that she cares about him, over and above her professional duties. "What do you suppose that means?" she asks.

He draws a long breath and lets it out. "I guess it means it's not time to open the champagne."

•

The painting is the best he has ever done. His intuition about using a primitive style was right. By flattening perspective he has mysteriously enlarged the depth of field, created a dreamlike sense of infinity in his visual space. The uniformity of the apple trees and the tigers is eerie, as is the contrast between the orderly calm of the orchard and the grinning rows of tiger teeth.

But the focal point is the man at the edge of the horizon. Zack has recently changed him, painted a flesh-and-blood hand on his shadow arm. The man seems to be breaking through the boundary between life and death to reach for Zack. In his memory, if it is a memory, he has seen his father's hand, big and square-knuckled with short, clean nails. The hand that tapped him and told him to get back inside the car. If he could remember more, he would paint the whole man at the edge of that orchard.

When he looks at the painting now, he can feel the yearning ache of his dreams. Maybe Nancy is right. Maybe he does desperately want and need a father. Maybe he is inventing the whole thing. It's funny. He thinks of his mother's description of his father, and it seems completely incompatible with his mental image. An unemployed busboy with a weak heart? Zack has a sense of someone strong and vital and far too intelligent to work only at odd jobs. Maybe he is fantasizing. The thought makes him feel hollow.

Clara has come up behind him and is looking at the painting. Mr. Taylor gave them permission to work late in the art room; he asked that they lock the door and drop the key in his mailbox. Mr. Taylor would do anything for them at this point because of the astonishing work they are producing. Once, Zack was his only star pupil, but now Clara comes close. It will be a toss-up who will take first place in the Spring Art Show next week.

"Are you religious?" she asks him.

He turns around, surprised. "No, not really. Why?"

She studies the canvas. "It just occurred to me. The Garden of Eden. Apple trees? And look how much your tiger tails are like snakes in the branches."

Zack doesn't like this explanation, but he has to consider it. "Shouldn't there be some naked people somewhere?" he jokes weakly.

"Maybe this is after they were cast out. Maybe that ghost in the background is the angel with the flaming sword."

"Ghost!" Zack shudders. "Why did you call him a ghost?"

"Well, phantom. Whatever he is. Oh, look! He's got a human hand! When did that happen?"

"Today. But I don't want to explain it, okay?"

"You don't have to. But am I right? Is it something religious?"

"I don't . . . think so." He feels profoundly confused. What if all this father stuff is a search for God? He remembers when he was a little boy in Sunday school. The teacher told him he should pray to his Father in heaven. Zack took it literally. For months he prayed to Anthony Lloyd instead of God. "I don't know what the hell it is," he says wearily. "Let's look at yours."

Clara's canvas is even more disturbing than Zack's. It is cold and lonely and . . . silent. Of course, all paintings are silent, but hers has a loud silence, like the moment in a party when everyone stops talking. In the foreground is the trestle of a high bridge, and somehow Clara has created an extraordinary distance down to the water, which is silvery and cold-looking. A sea gull hangs in the air under the bridge. The sky is a steely lilac-gray. She is painting something terrible. Zack is always frightened by this painting, and today he decides to give her a hard time. "Now this is a religious painting," he says. "Look at all the cross beams in the bridge. And that bird with his wings out, that's more crucifixion imagery. Of course, everyone knows that water symbolizes—"

"All right, all right." She laughs. "I guess you can do it with any painting."

"Your painting scares me," Zack says.

She looks at him with her thoughtful dark eyes. "Yours scares me."

They just look at each other. It occurs to Zack that he feels close to her, even though she's almost a stranger. Somehow they seem to understand each other without much explanation.

She breaks the spell. "I almost forgot! I brought that poem for you!" She rummages her huge tote bag and brings out a book of poems by William Blake. "The tiger poem I was telling you about," she says. "Remember?" She flips through the pages. "Here."

The poem is called "The Tiger." He reads it over and over, mesmerized. It is the most beautiful, disturbing thing he's ever read. One line in particular haunts him: "Did he who made the Lamb make thee?" That line somehow makes him think of Joshua. He shivers.

Clara stares at him. "I didn't mean to upset you," she says.

He shakes his head. "No. Do I look upset? I'm not upset, just . . . I don't know. I feel . . . I love this poem."

She smiles. "You can keep the book if you want to."

"Could I?" He wants to read the poem over and over. He wants to picture that beautiful, powerful beast.

"Of course," she says. "It's my first present to you."

He smiles. "Then I should give you something." He didn't really mean it to be suggestive, but it came out that way.

"Feel free." She looks boldly into his eyes.

He realizes how alone they are in this empty school-room, how late in the afternoon it is. All the voices in the halls have died away. The light slanting through the window is a deep gold. He has the key to the room. They could lock the door. . . .

He feels weak all over. He's not ready. Something about this girl is so overpowering, she could engulf him like a fire. He just isn't ready. He clears his throat and turns away, walking back toward his canvas.

"I wasn't trying to be pushy," she says.

"You're not." He refuses to look at her. "It's me. I'm . . . weird." He looks at his painting and feels cold. Maybe the thing to do is to tell her everything. Maybe that's what's wrong. He turns to her suddenly. "Tell me about your painting," he says.

She is looking at him coldly. "No."

"Please."

"No."

"You can trust me. If it's a secret, I'll never tell anyone."

"I know that."

"Then . . ."

"I don't like to talk about . . . stuff like that."

"Stuff like what?"

"Bad stuff. It makes it worse. The more you dwell on things— Just leave me alone, Zack. Are you going to tell me what your painting is all about?"

"I would if I could! But I don't know what it's about!"

She folds her arms. "You know more than you're telling."

He stiffens. "All right. I do. I think it's about my father. He died when I was five, and somehow I squelched all my memories of him. And now I think these nightmares are my memories coming back."

"He's the man in the shadows?"

"I think so. I think . . . some things are coming back to me about him. I think he had a red car and big hands and this beautiful voice. I've had little . . . like flashbacks."

"Wow," she says. "Did you love him a lot?"

To Zack's horror, tears fill his eyes. "Yes," he whispers. And in that moment he knows it's true. He adored his father. He worshiped him. Zack takes deep breaths and pushes the emotions down.

Clara just watches. She makes no move to come toward him or comfort him. When he is calm, she says, "I thought people blocked out only bad memories."

"Well, he *died*," Zack says. "I guess I couldn't handle it."

"Wow. I wonder why it's coming back to you now."

"I don't know. Because I'm growing up? Mom said he looked like me. Maybe now I'm looking in the mirror and seeing him." He remembers the legend on the car mirror. *Objects in the mirror are closer than they appear.*

"Wow," she says again.

"Now tell me about the bridge."

She looks away. "Uh-uh."

"Why?"

"It's different, Zack. Trust me."

But he doesn't. It isn't fair. He told her everything and this is how she repays him. "I'd understand, no matter what it is."

"I know. Try to understand why I don't want to talk about it."

"Well, I don't!" He can hear how he sounds, like a pouty two-year-old. Still, he can't help it. "It isn't *fair!*" he adds.

She laughs. "Now Zachary . . ." She walks toward him.

"Don't!" he says, pulling back. Worse than a sulky kid now. More like an old maiden aunt afraid of being violated.

"Don't be colicky," she chides. Close now, she reaches up and ruffles his hair.

He pushes her away gently. "Stop it. I mean it." He realizes, dimly, this is turning him on—acting distant and making her come after him. Nancy would have a field day with this.

She pulls him into her arms. He feels all her softness pressing against him. "You better be a good boy," she whispers teasingly. "Or I'll have to spank you." To demonstrate, she gives him a couple of gentle pats on the bottom.

Oh boy. He squirms, fighting the hardest rush of desire he has ever felt in his life. It's like something twisting inside him down there. It's like some animal that wants to be let out. She would let him, he knows it. She would let him here and now, right on the floor of the Temple of Art.

"Listen," he pants softly. "You better back off because . . ." He tries to pull back, but she holds him firmly, tips her face up and kisses his mouth. He feels dizzy, hot, drowning in lilacs. He wants to see her naked. He wants her. Now. His hands go all over her body, exploring, caressing. Something foreign and rebellious takes over in him. They start unfastening each other's clothes. He feels helpless. It's going to happen. It has to happen.

But when they get down to underwear, they both hesitate. He stares at her. Her lingerie is womanly, satiny, expensive-looking. A pale mauve trimmed in lace. The bra and panties match. The body they reveal is even more lush and curvy than he had imagined. And in her eyes he can see she's looking at him the same way, seeing whatever women see in men. He has never seen a girl really aroused. Tracy let him do things, but she always seemed a little bored, like a referee watching the game to make sure all the rules were followed. Clara is hot, breathing hard, sweeping her eyes over him. What is he waiting for? But he's scared. He can't help it. He's scared.

"We shouldn't," he mutters, hating himself.

"It's okay," she says impatiently. "I want to. Come on."

He doesn't look at her. "Somebody might catch us. A . . . janitor or something."

The hot look fades from her eyes. He's safe now. "You're right," she says. "Anyway, you aren't . . . protected, are you?"

He feels himself blush. He never thought of that. He has never been close enough to the real thing to even deal with that issue. He doesn't know anything about those things. "No," he says.

"Zack . . . you're a virgin, aren't you?"

His blush gets worse. Still, it would be stupid to lie. What if he lied and she could tell somehow? That would be worse. "Yes." He hangs his head.

"Well, don't look like *that*," she says. "It's no disgrace. It's just that . . . you know . . . I'm *not*."

"I figured that," he says, and regrets it instantly.

"What does that mean?"

"Nothing! It's just obvious that you . . . know what you're doing."

"Oh. Well, you were acting like you knew what you were doing too."

"Well, I do! I mean. I've done some stuff, you know? Just not . . . you know."

"I know." She smooths his hair. "No wonder you're a little spooked. You don't want to do your first time like this. Your first time should be special."

Things are starting to heat up and twist again. "Yeah?" he says faintly.

She kisses him. "Let's have a special date, you know? Make it really romantic. Really nice."

"Nice," he agrees, kissing her neck. His fingertips find a lace edge and work their way under.

"Zachary!" She laughs, pushing him away. "What did I just say?"

"I heard you!" he says, pulling himself together. "Nice and romantic."

She laughs, gets up and starts putting clothes on. He has to swallow hard so he won't cry, seeing all that lovely flesh disappear.

"My parents are going out of town in a couple of weeks. You can come over. I'll cook dinner for you. Want to? How does that sound?"

"Romantic," he says, gazing at her. "Nice."

Fully clothed, she comes and hugs him. "Put your pants on, you bad boy," she says. He grabs her and kisses her forcefully. He has a little frustration to work out. When he finally lets her go, she is dazed and panting.

He grins. "I guess I am a bad boy," he says.

She smiles happily. "I guess so."

He stays up late that night, reading the poems she has given him, about lambs and lost children and monstrous flowers and prophetic dreams.

EIGHT

Zack wins. It's funny. This year he feels bad about it, wishes his painting could have come in second to Clara's. After all, he won last year. But she gets a red ribbon, so at least they're united in being the two best artists in the school.

Winning this year has made Zack stop to think. He wonders how good he really is. He has always figured himself a "modest little talent," kind of like Mr. Taylor, who would end up teaching and painting quietly on the side. Maybe illustrating children's books or designing greeting cards. His favorite fantasy is that he has a big house on Cape Cod. He has never been to Cape Cod, but it *sounds* right. He has a beautiful Italian-American wife (Clara will do nicely) and a studio with a huge bay window on the ocean. They have no children (Zack can't imagine being a father), and they breed and train golden retrievers. Every morning Zack takes his dogs for a run on the beach. Then he goes to his studio and paints. Clara, who is painting in some other part of the house (he likes solitude when he works), brings him sandwiches and cappuccino from time to time. Every night she makes him stuffed shells or manicotti for dinner, fulfills his wildest sexual fantasies, and sleeps cozily by his side under a large down comforter strewn with dogs and puppies. Zack's whole life is a steady curve of unbroken comfort and peace. Nothing out of the way ever happens. Then, when he's dead, his widow (imagine Clara in a black lace veil!) takes all his paintings to New York and the galleries snap them up and Zack assumes his place in art history with no fuss or bother. Perfection.

But maybe, he thinks now, that fantasy is wrong. What if he's a bona fide genius? Maybe he should be aiming for New York right now. His plans for after graduation seem a little shabby in view of this spectacular painting he has made. With his SAT scores he could have chosen from among the best colleges, and with his portfolio he could storm any academy. But he has enrolled at Broward Community College because they had a family discussion and it had seemed the *sensible* thing to do. It was cheaper than going away. Mom implied she would miss him and need him. Josh didn't want him to go. Zack, for his part, couldn't imagine leaving the dog. He told himself a good artist can matriculate anywhere or not even go to college at all. The work is what's important.

But still . . . now he will be rubbing elbows with students who just want to decorate beach houses when they graduate, or get a corporate job designing cows to go on milk cartons. Is that an atmosphere that will push him to new heights?

He thinks it all over as he tries not to vomit, leads his

mother and brother into the sickening fluorescence that is Taravella High at night.

Of course what really bothers him is the pressure of having his mother here to judge his artwork, to see for herself what her son's blue ribbon is all about. Tonight she wears gray, not as pretty as the dress she wore for Josh's recital . . . But Nancy has made Zack swear he will curb that kind of thinking.

Zack knows he's out of control tonight. He has been doing breathing exercises since five o'clock, and it doesn't help. "Most of the paintings are here in the hall," he says. "Let's look at them first. Then we can go to the art room and see the prizewinners."

"All right," Mom and Josh say in unison. Such agreeable people. Josh has already seen the stuff many times, but like a good soldier, he walks solemnly along, letting Zack point out paintings he likes. Students and parents circle around them.

"This is dreck," Zack comments about a sophomore's watercolor of egrets in flight.

"Oh, but it's so beautiful!" Mom objects. She looks washed out in this light. Gray is not her color.

"Beautiful has nothing to do with it," Zack explains. "What if a chef baked a cake that looked beautiful but had no flavor?"

"I guess we should suck on these pictures and see what they taste like," Josh jokes. He is currently distracted by Katy Wincannon, a busty freshman who is showing her high-tech dad her miserable drawing of a cat. The dad looks like he's planning his next phone call.

"Excuse me a minute," says Josh, and heads for disaster.

"She's a bitch," Zack comments. "He hasn't got a chance."

"Please don't use words like that," Mom says, losing interest in the art as she watches her baby attempt a pickup. Josh barges over and is obviously singing the praises of the miserable cat. High-tech Dad looks as if they had been approached by a palmetto bug. Katy makes a routine visual sweep of Josh, discerns he is not any kind of big man on campus, and turns away.

Josh returns dejected. "What am I doing wrong?" he asks Zack.

"I could write a book about it," Zack tells him.

"Is Clara coming tonight?" Josh asks, slipping into the more comfortable role of living vicariously through Zack.

"I guess so." It is not a pleasant thought. Mom has never met her. He somehow wishes she never would. It is too much to have Mom judging his painting and his girlfriend all in one night. He feels very naked.

"Look at this." He points to a drawing. "This is my likely successor. He's only a freshman, but look at the sense of line." At least when he talks art, they both shut up. They haven't a clue what he is saying.

Slowly, breathing deeply, Zack leads his family up the hall toward the art room where Mr. Taylor will be presiding over the three prizewinning paintings. Every so often he has to stop and say hi to another student he knows. All of them treat him like the celebrity he is. Mom and Josh seem impressed.

As they approach the art room he hears Clara's liquid laugh. The gods hate him. He's going to be completely naked in front of his mother. He takes a deep breath and leads them in.

Mr. Taylor has arranged the three winning paintings on easels at the front of the room. Clara's bridge and a warped, Van Goghish self-portrait of a girl in the junior class flank Zack's magnificent "Tiger Orchard," which now sports a blue ribbon. Mr. Taylor is perched on the corner of the desk. He drinks coffee from a paper cup as he talks to Clara and her father. Clara, playing the art student tonight, is all in black, with masses of gold crosses and chains. Zack is aroused at once, remembering their moment of passion right here in this room and picturing her mauve and lace splendor. Under this outfit she must surely have black lace. He just knows it. He wants to bite her perfectly rounded shoulder through the stretchy material of her dress. Their sex-date is set for a week from today, the night before graduation. Graduation has taken on a whole new meaning for him.

Mr. Benedetto, a plumber, looks up and sees Zack. There is no joy in his stare. Zack has met Clara's parents several times at the door when he goes to pick her up. The welcome has never been warm, but Zack feels that goes with the territory. Mr. B. is a short man with a powerful, dense body and heavy eyebrows. The eyebrows are low now, drawn down to protect his daughter from Zack's evil hormones.

Mr. Taylor follows the angry stare. "Zack!" he cries lovingly. "Come over here. Let me get my two prizewinners together."

Zack moves forward, mother and brother in his wake. He notices his mother doesn't even glance at his painting. She is looking at the cross in Clara's ear.

"I was just telling Mr. Benedetto what a remarkable year this has been for me as a teacher," Mr. Taylor gushes, oblivious to crosscurrents. "Having two such promising students. That very rarely happens."

No one pays any attention to this. Zack and Clara are looking at each other. Josh and Mom are staring at Clara, the one with lust, the other disapproval. Mr. Benedetto trains his gaze on Zack, like an attack dog.

"Where's your mom?" Zack says quietly.

"She has the flu," says Mr. Benedetto, as if it might be Zack's fault.

Mr. Taylor looks mildly puzzled, then turns to Mrs. Lloyd. "Come and see the artwork," he prompts, jumping off his desk. Everyone troops after him. "This is our third-place winner, Laura Davis," he says, like a master of ceremonies. "The juniors all did self-portraits."

"It looks like a badly adjusted TV," says Mrs. Lloyd. She, Josh, and Mr. Benedetto laugh.

"Well," Mr. Taylor says uneasily. "I think she's trying to show that her life is out of kilter in some way."

"Young people are so serious," says Mrs. Lloyd.

Mr. Taylor blinks several times but is undaunted. He has dealt with Zack's mother before and already has low expectations. "And this is Clara's painting, of course," he continues. "The seniors are painting their darkest secrets. The assignment was to reveal and conceal at the same time."

Mr. Benedetto suddenly turns away and walks to a window. Clara looks after him coldly.

Mrs. Lloyd gazes at Clara's painting thoughtfully. "What a pretty bird!" she says. "Is that a sea gull?"

Clara's eyebrows disappear somewhere in her hair. "Yes," she says.

Zack feels better. Clara is getting the same level of understanding he usually gets. Not only has his mom missed the whole mood of the painting; her dad apparently can't even stand to look at her work. He is resting his fists on the windowsill now, gazing at the stars. Clara glowers at his back.

"And here," Mr. Taylor says with ill-concealed pride, ". . . is 'The Tiger Orchard.'"

Mrs. Lloyd looks at Zack's painting as if it had been invisible until the moment it was pointed out to her. "Oh, my!" she says. She gazes and gazes without a word. "Oh, my!" she says again.

Zack's whole body has turned on him. He's blushing, sweating, fidgeting. His stomach is churning. His head hurts. His heart is beating crazily. *Say something!* he screams in his head. *Just say something!*

She turns bland blue eyes to Zack. "What is it supposed to be?"

He is naked in Times Square. He is caught in a prison searchlight. He is onstage at Lincoln Center. "It's a tiger orchard," he says with weak defiance. "Where they grow tigers."

"I mean—" she begins.

"He can't tell you what it means," Mr. Taylor interrupts. "It's his secret. That's the assignment."

"Oh." She makes it clear what she thinks of the giver of such an assignment.

"Do you like it?" Zack hears himself cry. His voice is too loud, too high. Even Mr. B. turns from the window.

She returns her thoughtful gaze to the painting. She gently hugs herself, as if chilled. "It's so *frightening*."

Zack is mute with despair. He wants to scream in her face. Can't she just say he's a good painter? That she's proud? Would that kill her? Did she complain when Josh played that depressing dead-leaf music? No! She just talked about his talent. Zack's frustration runs through his body like shivers, like a cold gust of wind. He cannot look at or speak to anyone. She has let him down.

Even Mr. Taylor senses the party is not on track. "It's a very powerful work," he says to Mrs. Lloyd.

She doesn't answer. She just stares at the picture. Mr. Benedetto keeps looking out the window. Josh is gazing at the third-place painting, now noticing that the girl in it has breasts. Zack and Clara exchange a look of sympathy that draws them closer than any physical bond ever could.

"It's gallery-quality!" Mr. Taylor shouts into the wind.

•

She means well. Zack grips the steering wheel with white fingers as they drive home through the starlight. She just didn't say the right words. Of course she's proud of him. He can control his anger, channel it into understanding. He has never had a real fight with his mother, and he's proud of it. Nancy couldn't believe it when he told her. *Everyone fights with their parents,* she had said. *It's a developmental necessity.*

Not for me, Zack had said. He hates the idea of fighting with her. It would be like making tracks in fresh snow or smashing expensive china. The damage would be irreparable. She would never forgive him.

So breathe deep and think good thoughts. After all, she stared at the canvas a long time. Obviously it moved her. She just can't verbalize it. Still, she could have said something about the ribbon. If Josh had won a prize . . .

"Zack, you're accelerating," she says quietly.

He feels slapped. But she's right, the needle is creeping up. Meekly he eases up on the gas.

"What did you think of Clara, Mom?" Josh asks from the backseat.

"She seems nice enough. I liked her father. He seemed like a good, decent man."

"He shouldn't have walked away from Clara's painting," Zack says. "He hurt her."

"Young people are so sensitive," she murmurs. "Does she always dress that way?"

Zack slides his eyes toward her. "What way?"

"I suppose that's the style, isn't it? But that dress was a little tight on her."

"It sure was!" Josh agrees with enthusiasm.

"She has a very pretty face," Mrs. Lloyd continues. "If she lost a little weight—"

"What are you talking about?" Zack explodes, resolution forgotten. "She's not fat! She's perfect! She's absolutely perfect!"

"And then some," says Josh.

"Why don't you shut the hell up?" Zack shouts at him.

"Zachary!" says Mrs. Lloyd. "Don't talk that way to your brother."

"I'm not a little kid!" Zack says. "Don't tell me how to talk to people!"

"Obviously," she says, remaining outwardly calm, "you need to be told."

"I didn't mean to make you mad, Zack," Josh says anxiously. "I think Clara's beautiful. She's got a gorgeous body!"

"Please don't speak disrespectfully!" Mrs. Lloyd says to Josh. She turns to Zack. "Is she a Catholic?"

"Is there something wrong with that?" Zack asks in a soprano voice.

"I'm just asking questions! Why are you biting my head off?"

"I'm not!" Zack wails. "But your questions are so— Mom, sometimes you really hurt me without meaning to!" *Okay, don't panic. That's good. That's honest communication. Nancy would approve.*

"Oh?" She looks royally miffed. "When is that?"

He feels helpless, like a foreigner struggling with English. "Well, like tonight for instance. My painting. That's like the biggest thing in my whole year. That's probably the best work I've done in my life. I was the best in the whole school. Mr. Taylor thinks I have a lot of potential."

"Sweetheart, I know all that."

"But Mom, you just gaped at it. You didn't say anything good about it."

"I wouldn't know what to say. I don't really understand art."

"Well, it's not like calculus. You don't have to be an artist to look at a painting and react to it. You were looking at it like it was some kind of horrible car accident!"

"You guys . . ." Josh is squirming in the backseat like someone who's about to wet his pants. He hates fights even worse than they do.

"What did you expect me to say?" she asks. "It's a frightening painting. Why would you paint something like that?"

"It's me!" He thumps his chest. "That's me! I have to paint what's inside me!"

91

"Watch the road," she tells him. "I don't think that painting is you at all. You're a perfectly nice boy."

"What does that mean? I should paint a plate of muffins or something? Don't you think there are things inside all of us—"

"No, I do not," she says. "And I know where these ideas are coming from too."

He is lost. "Huh?"

She turns to him. Her mouth is tightly compressed. "It's this therapist. This Nancy. She's filled your head with crazy ideas. You used to be the calmest, sweetest little boy and now you're having bad dreams and shouting at everyone and painting horrible animals!"

"I had the dreams before I started therapy! That's why I started therapy! To get at these things inside me!"

"Well, I certainly don't think your therapy is doing you any good!" she says. "You never spoke to me this way before. Maybe whatever is inside you ought to stay there. Suddenly you're sullen and defiant and you want to see this girl who dresses in black leather—"

"She wasn't wearing leather! She didn't have one stitch of leather!"

"You guys!" Josh whines like a frightened puppy.

"You've become a complete stranger," she says. "I don't even know you."

Zack stares at the road ahead. "You never did," he says bitterly.

•

At home it is Josh who can't let the fight go. Zack and his mother spend a few hours watching TV in stony silence, and their anger wears off. Zack doesn't think he will forget this, but he wants to forgive. Around ten she offers him ice cream and he accepts. A truce. Nothing solved, but a good papering-over. The best they can do.

But Joshua is spooky and silent and lets his ice cream melt into pink soup. Zack tries not to notice, irritated at the prospect of having to dredge all this up again in their room.

Sure enough, when he comes out of the bathroom, bone-weary, and stoops to kiss the dog, Joshua whispers from the shadows, "Why do you have to make her mad like that?"

Zack flops on the bed, waits for the bounce of Beamer jumping aboard, and settles into a comfortable position. He isn't up to this. He wants to picture Clara in black lace underwear and develop the thought into a full-scale bedtime story. "Ask her why she has to make me so mad," he counters.

A long silence. "Zack?" Josh's voice is small, like a child's. "Maybe you shouldn't go to that doctor anymore. Everything was okay around here until you started that."

Zack sighs, and Beamer rushes up to lick his face. Zack pushes him away gently. "It wasn't okay for me," he says, and realizes this is true. It isn't even just the nightmares. There's been something bad inside him all his life that needs to come out.

"Why do you act like you've got something against

her?" Josh says. "I don't think we could ask for a better mother. After all she's been through, having to raise us all alone. You know?"

"I know. I didn't say she was a bad mother, did I?"

"You act like she is."

Zack sits up, losing his fatigue in the heat of this new battle. Beamer sits up too. "She acts like I'm a bad son! Can't you see that?"

"No. Not at all."

"She does. She acts like I'm the enemy, and do you know why? It's because I look like *him.*"

"Who?"

"Our father. She hates me for reminding her of him. That's why she hates my therapy. Because my dreams are about him and I'm remembering him and she wants to leave him dead and buried!" Zack feels he's being brilliant. He has reached the very core of his problem. He thinks of writing all this down for Nancy.

Then he hears a little sob in the darkness. Soft at first, then loud and uninhibited. Like a little boy, Josh wails, his hands covering his face.

Automatically Zack and Beamer go to him. Zack puts his hand on Josh's wildly jerking shoulder. "What's wrong?" Zack asks. "What brought this on?"

Josh almost seems to be choking to death. He grabs his brother as if his life depends on it. "I don't know!"

NINE

Zack has died and gone to paradise. He is sitting in a Mediterranean-style living room whose green and gold accents are a delicious contrast to his mother's house of brown and blue. He has fallen in love with a sideboard whose glass doors are inlaid with filigree. On top are candlesticks and an embellished bottle such as a genie might come out of. He can hear his mother's tongue clicking. *All that gold*, she would murmur, as if gold were not something to rejoice and be glad in.

Zack is glad. He is in his full fantasy mode. This house no longer belongs to Mr. and Mrs. Joe Benedetto. It belongs to him and Clara. It is their villa in Naples, like the one he saw recently on *Lifestyles of the Rich and Famous*. He was all wrong about Cape Cod. They will live on the Riviera and drink their morning coffee on a circular terrace with steep marble steps that descend to the sea. His painting will become richer, wilder, like Rousseau. Like the poems of William Blake. He will stand at his easel every day, shirtless and barefoot. His mother will be scandalized.

Clara comes from the kitchen, an angel tonight in a white sundress that emphasizes her tan and her dark, lustrous curls. She wears no lipstick, just mascara. She carries a glass of dark/red wine.

"Sure you don't want the TV on?" she asks.

"Oh no!" Zack says. Who would watch *Wheel of Fortune* in an Italian villa?

"It'll be about fifteen more minutes," she says. "The sauce has to reduce. I thought you'd like some wine." She offers the glass the way Eve must have held out the apple.

Like Adam, he hesitates. He has never been fond of alcohol. In fact, he has a deep fear and mistrust of it. After all, he has to drive home. But tonight it's so much a part of the atmosphere. It's not very Neapolitan to ask for ginger ale. Anyway, later on he might be making love to a girl with more experience than him. A little nerve tonic wouldn't hurt.

"Thank you," he says softly, taking the glass. It is room temperature, not cold, and dark and soft as rose petals. He sips thoughtfully.

She has perched on the arm of a green and gold chair, her skirt poufed out and revealing beautiful legs. *Why do we have to eat dinner?* he thinks.

"What kind of dressing do you want on your salad?" she asks.

He marvels at her cool. She knows as well as he does where this evening is headed. When he asked her on the phone yesterday if he could bring something, she said, with a giggle, "Condoms." Women are fearless.

"Italian," he says, breathing in the olive and garlic aroma of the kitchen. "I love everything Italian."

96

"Flatterer." She hops up from her perch and comes to him, leans over, pecks his cheek. Her fluffy skirt, inches away, taunts him. If only it would catch on something and give him a quick peek. If he were bolder, he would reach underneath, but by the time he has the courage, she has swished back into the kitchen.

He takes a sip of wine to steady himself. He'd better keep himself on a low simmer or he'll never make it through dinner. But the wine isn't helping. He wonders what color underwear she's chosen for tonight. Red? Black? Maybe white to match her dress. Maybe she has white panties with ruffles across the bottom such as little girls wear . . .

"Dinner is served!" she calls.

He limps to the dining room.

•

During dinner his mood shifts away from sex and he feels romantic, just plain romantic. But that's not quite it either. He feels comforted, soothed, complete. The dining room is lit by candles whose flames have expanded to warm, hovering halos in his semidrunken state. The air is rich with the aromas of fresh bread and roasted garlic. Clara is glorious by candlelight, her lashes casting deep shadows on her cheeks when she looks down. Her gold charm bracelet catches the candlelight and splinters it like fireworks across the table. And there's the wine, a deeply consoling, lulling thing—cherry bark and nutmeg. He feels like a child drowsing through a beautiful bedtime story. Perhaps they talk but he doesn't remember. He remembers the scene as silent, like a dream. And at the right moment she pushes back her chair and holds out her hand and leads him down the hall to her bedroom.

She lights more candles here. Everything sways. He knows he is drunk, prays it won't make a difference. But in a way he is glad. For once, he won't mess things up with his endless worries and doubts. All he can do now is go along.

He sees her painting, still with its prize ribbon, propped up in a corner. It frightens him. He looks away. He turns instead at the soft glint of the objects on her dressing table. Perfume bottles and hairbrushes and little boxes. She's a woman. Someday they will live together and these pretty little things will be a part of his life.

He looks at her now as she turns from the last candle and waves out the match. He circles her with his arms and kisses her. This is easy. This is going to be easy. They take a long time with the kiss, one last moment together as strangers. Then he unzips her dress and runs his hand down her back. It is a smooth, unbroken line. No bra. Trembling, he moves his hand lower. No panties. "Oh God," he whispers.

She laughs and unbuckles his belt.

•

He speeds like a comet on the highway. He is above all laws now, the laws of physics, the laws of Florida, his mother's moral code. His graduation is coming early. He's a man and he doesn't have to scuttle around like a scared kid anymore.

Not only a man but a man in love. The part they don't tell you about is the moment *after* sex, when everything quiets down and you realize it wasn't just bodies that touched, it was souls. His soul has touched Clara's and now they know each other in a secret way that joins them for eternity. Even if they don't stay together, they will still be a part of each other.

He feels ashamed for every moment he ever wasted on earth being unhappy. How could he? When his life is nothing but a shower of miracles. His art. His girl. The stars. The highway. The joy of being alive in a beautiful, physical world.

The lane ahead is clear. Just for one moment he wants to take off and fly, push it to the limit. He presses the accelerator down, feels the wind rush into his face . . .

It wails. It rises and falls. Zack topples from his mystic ecstasy as fast as his car decelerates from ninety-five to fifty-five. But it doesn't matter. He pushed it too far. A cruiser from hell is flying toward him like the Invisible Worm. Like the hornet that stung his mother on the hand once and paralyzed her fingers for days. "You never see them coming," she had said.

He sees the cruiser now, flashing and wailing as if trying to pull over Al Capone. Zack knows he was wrong. It isn't such a great world. We are punished for every moment of joy. He will be arrested, booked, fingerprinted.

Put on the eleven o'clock news, strip-searched, body-searched, locked away forever. It is right before his graduation and he might very well be drunk. His mother will find out he's a drunk, a reckless driver, a fornicator. It was always his destiny. He should have known. He pulls over and waits as the flash and wail draw closer and closer.

He does not even look up at the officer. He thinks he might be on the verge of crying.

"May I see your license, please?" Contralto. He looks up, startled to see a black braid hanging over the uniformed shoulder. He is going to be booked by a woman.

He pulls out his license and hands it over. His fingers are trembling.

"Is this your current address, Zachary?" she asks.

Until he is kicked out. "Yes, ma'am."

"You were driving above the speed limit. I clocked you at eighty-eight."

"I know."

"Would you step out of the car, please."

He steps out. He is shaking so badly, he can hardly stand.

"Have you been drinking, Zachary?" Her tone is so strange. Kind of like an automated teller machine. Friendly, but not really.

"Yes," he says, barely audible.

"How much have you had to drink?"

"Two glasses of wine." He hangs his head.

For some reason she laughs. "Are you sure that's all?"

"Yes."

"How long ago was that?"

"About four hours ago. Around six."

"Nothing else since then? Not even a beer or anything?"

"No, ma'am."

"Okay. I want you to walk for me. One foot directly in front of the other. Just like this." She demonstrates, looking for all the world like a little girl on a balance beam. To his utter shame, he's aware that he finds her attractive.

Zachary walks. He doesn't stumble or fall, but suddenly he starts thinking about all the cars passing them on the interstate, hundreds of strangers watching him take a sobriety test. What are the odds someone will go past who knows him? He suddenly chokes up, and even though he fights like hell to control it, a kind of sob rises from his throat. He tries not to look at the officer as he struggles with himself.

"Do you want to sit down?" she says kindly.

He nods, sits sideways in his car, covers his face. He doubts very much she is going to believe his two-drink story now.

"I'm going to go make a call," she says. "I'll be right back." She walks to the cruiser and begins talking on her radio. Zack figures she is getting reinforcements, maybe some people from one of those "retreats" for teenagers where they take you to a duck pond and straighten you out.

She talks a long time, which allows Zack to get a grip on himself. He knows his life is ruined, but he's glad that at least he had one perfect night with Clara. That will be something to think about in the penitentiary.

Finally she returns. "Feeling better?" she asks.

"Yes. Thank you."

She laughs again. Zack seems to amuse her. "Were you coming from a party?"

"No. I was at my girlfriend's. We were having dinner because our graduation's tomorrow. I guess that's why I was speeding. I just felt good . . ." He trails off. It sounds stupid.

"You shouldn't endanger other people just because you feel good. You'd better learn to whistle or sing or something."

He laughs gratefully. "Yes, ma'am."

"Will you tell me something? What made you so upset just now?"

He looks up, pleadingly. "I just don't want to get a ticket. I know I was wrong and I deserve it, but my mother. She'd be so disappointed in me. I'm like . . . I don't do things like that. I'm an honor student and my graduation is tomorrow. I don't want her to think I'm some kind of— She depends on me for stuff. My father is dead . . ." His voice is about to break, and he cuts himself off. Of all the stupid ramblings. . . .

"Okay," she says. "I think I see. Well, look. As far as I can tell you're sober and I don't think you're the type who would lie about things. In fact, you seem like a pretty honorable guy. So I'm just going to give you a warning."

"Oh, thank you!"

"Wait a minute. I didn't give you the warning yet. I want you to make a promise to me. I want you to give me your word you won't drive above the posted limit ever again. I know it seems like fun sometimes and you think you've got it under control, but if you could see what I've seen. Kids your age that plow into another car and maybe kill somebody or maim them. Then you have to live with that forever. My brother used to speed all the time, and one day he hit a dog and killed it. He still cries when he talks about it. You know what I mean?"

Zack hangs his head. He thinks of Beamer.

"So you do me a favor," she continues. "I won't cite you and you make it easier for society by not being a reckless fool. Deal?"

"Deal," he says. "Thank you."

She slaps his arm. "Happy graduation, Zachary."

He starts up and drives the rest of the way home as if the car and the road were electrified and one false move would fry him like a breaded shrimp.

•

By the time he gets home, exhaustion has set in. He is deeply relieved to find Joshua asleep. He isn't in the mood to give a blow-by-blow of his date. He isn't in the mood for anything except the dead blackness of sleep. He has had a little too much this evening, between love and terror. And tomorrow he has to graduate from high school. Zack takes off his clothes for the second time that night and slides between the sheets. Beamer, on the other bed, rouses himself, yawns, and leaves Josh to sleep with Zack. Zack strokes him mindlessly, closing his eyes, remembering Clara's warm lilac scent, seeing the flash of the patrol car, and then his mind unravels and he is drifting among stars.

•

He is tooling along the highway in his red Pinto, sleeves rolled up to the elbows, one arm out the window. The wind blows his hair. He is himself but older, a man in his thirties. He turns on the car radio. The Eagles are singing "Take It to the Limit."

"Your wish is my command," Zack says jauntily to the radio. He is not quite himself somehow. Cheerier. Cockier. More reckless. He presses the accelerator down hard, and the car shoots forward. Zack throws back his head and laughs. "Yes, Jesus!" he says. He is definitely not himself.

He rockets along a deserted highway through grass and trees that are clearly midwestern. He passes a vast apple orchard. The even rows pulse as he shoots by. Then comes a huge billboard with the legend *Objects in the mirror are closer than they appear*.

The sky is bright and blue. He feels happy. He lights a cigarette, something Zack is sure he will never do, and, worse, throws the match out the window. He snaps off the radio and sings songs from the score of *Peter Pan*.

He tosses the cigarette out the window. "This is the life." He sighs contentedly.

Suddenly there are patrol cars everywhere. Blocking the road ahead, coming up from behind, closing in across the fields on either side of the car. Zack's joy plummets to despair. "Why did I ever think I could get away with this?" he cries.

The Pinto slows to a stop, and all the cruisers close in, making a tight ring around him, flashing their lights until he is dizzy and blinded. Someone speaks through a megaphone. "Please step out of the car."

Slowly he opens the door and stands. The sunlight blinds him. He has no sunglasses. One by one, huge police officers get out of the cruisers. They all have sunglasses. They look like insects with their hard, polished lenses. From the last car Zack's mother emerges in a green flowered dress. Her face is stern and unforgiving and at the same time incredibly beautiful.

"Mary!" Zack calls to his mother. "Please don't do this to me!"

"You brought it on yourself," she says coldly. And as if this were the attack command, the officers all rush him at once, grabbing him, turning him around, slamming his face against the hood, sticking their hands in his pockets.

He hears a child behind him screaming. "Don't hurt him!"

"You be quiet!" his mother screams, and he hears a smack.

"Leave him alone!" Zack shouts, twisting himself upright, out of the policemen's grasp. "This isn't his fault!"

One of the cops grabs his hair and slams him down

again, harder than the first time. He is panicking now, struggling and screaming, but it does no good. They are clamping handcuffs on him, shoving him into the back of a car.

Later he wakes up in jail. But it isn't jail, it's the zoo. Rows and rows of cages. Across from him a tiger paces up and down. It catches his eye and stops, then lets out a roar of pure despair.

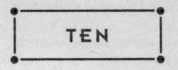

TEN

He wakes up with a brain full of fog. *Hangover*, he thinks rather proudly. He sits up in bed, moaning, touching his forehead, exaggerating each gesture. Beamer looks at him with alarm, but Josh, the intended audience, snoozes on like a baby, arms around his pillow and a foot sticking out of the sheets.

Zack is determined to put on a show. "Oh, God!" he says loudly.

Josh opens his eyes, rolls on his back, gazes at the ceiling. "What?"

"Be a brother and get me some aspirin, would you?" Zack whispers. He doesn't have a headache at all, really, just a funny, foggy feeling. But what the hell.

"Huh?" says Josh, who takes a long time to wake up. He finally looks over. "What's the matter?"

"Drank a bunch of wine," Zack says faintly. He is such a good actor, he's convincing himself. When he closes his eyes, the room seems to spin.

Finally Josh regains full consciousness and realizes the significance of his brother's headache. He climbs onto Zack's bed, crowding him. "What else happened?" he demands.

Zack is having a great time now. "Get me the aspirin first, please."

"Wow!" Josh scurries to the bathroom.

Left alone for a second, Zack explores his real feelings. Foggy. No other word for it. It's like he can't quite focus. There's something . . .

Josh is back, climbing onto the bed again, handing Zack his pills and water. Then he loops his arm around the dog and settles in. "So what happened?"

Onstage, Zack takes the aspirin with a single gulp. He runs his hands through his hair. "What a pervert you are!" he says. "What do you think happened?"

"I know what happened," Josh replies. "I just want the details."

"Well, a gentleman doesn't kiss and tell." Zack sips demurely at his water. This is really fun.

"Oh, please. Just the highlights."

Zack pretends to scrutinize his brother for worthiness. "Well, okay. I mean, how are you going to learn anything about life if I don't teach you?"

"That's right." Josh pulls up his knees and hugs them.

"Okay," Zack begins, struggling to control his own enthusiasm. "So I went to her house . . ."

"And her parents were out of town . . ."

"That's right. And she cooked fettuccine Alfredo for me and we ate dinner by candlelight and she gave me some kind of red wine to drink—"

"Did you get drunk?"

"Sort of. And then she took me to her room—"

108

"What do you mean? Did she say, 'Let's go to my room'?"

"No. She just got up from the table and held out her hand and led me."

"Oh, wow!"

"Yeah. And so we got to her room and she lit all these candles . . ."

"Were you turned on?"

"What do you think? And we started kissing and messing around—"

"What do you mean?"

"You know what I mean. And I unzipped her dress . . ."

"Yeah . . ."

"And . . ."

"Yeah . . ."

Zack drops to a whisper. "She wasn't wearing any underwear."

Josh whispers too. "Oh, God. Are you kidding?"

"Nope."

"Not *any*?"

"That's what I said."

Josh trembles a little. "You mean not even . . . like . . . her panties?"

"You got it."

"Oh, God!" Josh squirms. His face is bright pink. He takes a second to recover his composure. "Then what?"

"You know what."

"You really did?"

"Wouldn't you?"

"On the bed?"

"No. We did it on the ceiling."

"God. Was it . . ."

"Yes."

"I mean, is it . . ."

"It is. It was. It was great." Zack gives up his cool. He is just too much in love. "She . . . I can't say much more because, you know. I don't want to talk about her, but, you know, it was . . . like . . . incredible."

"Wow!" Josh is happy with the whole world. There is a Santa Claus after all. "Zack?" he asks coyly.

"What?"

"Was that the first time you ever . . . well . . ."

Zack is torn. He'd rather come off more worldly than he is, but maybe it's better to tell the truth. After all, the kid has nobody else to ask. "All the way like that, yeah."

Josh has another question. He opens his mouth and closes it.

"What?"

"Is there anything . . . well, you know . . . tricky about it? I mean is it pretty easy, the first time, to . . . you know . . . get it right?"

Zack laughs. He can remember yesterday when he was innocent like that. "Buddy," he says. "It's like falling off a log."

•

They drive to the graduation ceremony. Mom and Josh chat away in the front seat, but Zack is quiet. The foggy feeling won't go away. He realizes he has felt like this once before, when he had that first flashback of his father. Maybe he is about to remember something else. It is almost . . .

"Did you hear me?" his mother asks.

"Huh?"

She turns around. She looks beautiful in her best blue dress, which she wears just for him, and bright cherry-colored lipstick. "I said we should go out after the ceremony and celebrate."

He has an image of his old bedroom back in Ohio and wallpaper with a sailboat motif. And Josh crying. There is some kind of trouble in another room. Shouting.

"Yeah," he says vaguely, trying to hold the image. "That'd be great."

"Where do you want to go?" she asks. "Chili's?"

I've had enough! he hears her scream in his head. *You've used up all your second chances!* "Yeah, yeah, Chili's is fine."

He hears a man answer in a low voice. The last word is *Zachary.* Zack sees himself, a little boy getting out of his bed and going to the door to listen better.

"You can ask Theresa to come along too," his mother says.

"Clarissa!" he says with real anger. "And anyway she's busy!"

"Clarissa," his mother repeats nervously.

•

At the school it is almost impossible to get rid of them. They are supposed to go sit in the bleachers on the soccer field while Zack changes into his cap and gown, but his mother can't seem to let him go, as if this were some great and final parting.

"Make sure you put your hat on straight," she urges while Josh giggles.

"It's not a hat," Zack grumbles. He wants to be alone so he can think.

"And don't sit with your legs apart during the ceremony. It looks so awful when boys do that."

"Mother!"

Josh has hysterics.

"Don't forget to shake hands with your principal when he gives you your diploma. And smile."

Zack gives a macabre parody of a vivacious smile. "How's this?" he asks through his teeth.

She ignores this. "Let's take a picture before you go."

"Oh, jeez!"

"Stand with your brother," she says, tilting the camera crazily. Her pictures never come out. "Put your hand on his shoulder as if you're giving him some brotherly advice."

Zack plants his hand on Josh's shoulder. "Keep your powder dry," he says solemnly.

Josh, who thinks this is something dirty, trembles with

laughter. Mom snaps the picture with her hand over the lens. Zack makes his escape.

The graduates are supposed to suit up in the art room because it is spacious, but most of them head for the bathrooms where they can use mirrors. In the boys' room rowdiness takes over. The guys are grabbing one another's tassels and sticking them in the commodes or flying around like bats in their gowns. Zack has always been a well-respected island, though, so they genially exclude him from the horseplay. He tries his mortarboard this way and that, hoping for an angle that won't look stupid. There isn't one.

He thinks about his memory fragment again. His parents are fighting. That much he knows. He knows, somehow, that they fight all the time, especially after they put the boys to bed. Glass breaks sometimes and they yell, or rather Mom yells at Dad. She doesn't like him. He's . . . bad. He does something bad. Gets in trouble. Zack and Josh hear everything, and Josh cries while Zack lies in bed with his stomach twisting . . .

He focuses on his own reflection again. Both dignified and goofy, he decides. What a time for this stuff to be coming through! But it's interesting. He always thought his mother wouldn't talk about his father because she loved him so much and she was too broken up over his death to deal with it. But now he understands. It makes sense. The disdainful set of her mouth the last time she spoke of Dad. "He took a lot of odd jobs. Waited tables." She looked down on her husband. Zack isn't sure how that makes him feel. Angry. Scared. Strangely excited. He's finally caught her at something. Maybe there's more to her than meets the eye. Maybe under that placid, good-natured exterior . . .

He realizes the boys' room is emptying. It's time to go.

•

"Guess who?" A pair of hands, the softest, most talented lilac-scented hands in the world cover his eyes, and a luscious, familiar body presses against his back.

"Mrs. Troutwine?" he suggests. Mrs. Troutwine is a geriatric English teacher at Taravella.

"Let me give you a hint." She bumps her pelvis gently against him.

"That could be almost anybody!" he complains.

"Here's a better hint," she whispers in his ear. "I'm not wearing anything under my graduation gown."

He pulls away and spins around. "Are you kidding?" he snaps, imagining a sudden gust of wind on the soccer field exposing his private treasures to the world.

"See for yourself!" The brazen hussy lifts her gown and reveals a pair of red track shorts and a Mickey Mouse T-shirt.

He looks down at her wicked, laughing face. His lover's face. He forgets there's a roomful of other graduates and pulls her against him. "You're a bad girl," he whispers gratefully.

•

Talking to Clarissa dissipates the fog for a while, but when a troop of maniacally cheerful guidance counselors comes to organize them into a double row in alphabetical order, the mist fills his head like a drug. He keeps seeing a man's white oxford shirt with the sleeves rolled up to the elbows. His father! His father . . .

He has to concentrate as they march like convicts across the soccer field. The band plays something grim. Cameras are snapping like firecrackers. His mother is probably taking a whole series of pictures of some guy behind him in the line, and he smiles to himself.

Now he is comfortably settled on the bleachers, and there is nothing else to do but sit through the long, boring program. Zack takes a minute to realize what it all means. High school is over. He's free. College has to be better. He'll be studying what he wants to study instead of taking PE and cutting up frogs. He'll be with Clarissa. She enrolled at Broward Community College when she found out he was going there. They'll take the same classes, and sometimes they'll cut school and fool around in his house while Mom's at work.

The sky is so blue today and a fresh breeze is blowing. Zack feels happy. While Mr. Hirschhorn, the principal, makes his opening remarks, an egret lands on the field and shuffles around. The senior class nudges and giggles.

A priest is up next. Zack automatically looks down at his lap. "Father . . ." the priest begins.

Zack closes his eyes and suddenly he can see him. Not God but his father. Clear as anything. The fight is over and his father has come into the boys' room. He sits at the foot of Zack's bed. He wears brown corduroys and a white oxford shirt with the sleeves rolled up. He looks like Zack—the same oak-and-honey hair, the same prominent bridge in his nose, the same restless eyes. He is tall, tall, tall and has broad shoulders and large hands. His face tonight is scared and anxious. "How ya doin'?" he asks, and even though Zack is only five, he can tell it's an act. False confidence.

". . . to these our children, the hope of our future," concludes the priest. "Amen."

It was an important night, that night. Dad had something important to say that led to all the trouble . . . No, don't think about that yet.

Lynn Mavor, the class valedictorian, is up now. She looks witchy to Zack, but a lot of guys go for her. Zack smiles at Clara to show he's not one of them. "What will my generation do with this planet?" Lynn asks, as if the whole thing were up to her. Cameras snap crazily.

Zack timidly calls back the image of his father. Now it is easy. Once a memory comes through, it's there. He knows the night, remembers it. October. It is almost Halloween. The air smells like bonfires. His father is close to him. He smells of wood chips and cigarette smoke and stale beer. Zack loves this smell. He loves this man. He can remember being pulled into his father's lap by those big, strong hands and being cuddled. Dad adored him and he knew it. He could charm his father. And somehow his father always knew when something was bothering

116

him. Even sometimes when Zack himself didn't know. His father's voice, usually rich and smooth, is jumpy with emotion on this night. "Your mother wants me to leave," he says.

Zack is wide awake now, terrified. "Forever?"

His father shifts his eyes. "Sometimes this happens," he says.

Chauncey Davis gets up to sing "All Things Bright and Beautiful." Chauncey has rehearsed the song all week, and Zack has grown to hate it. Now he doesn't even hear it.

"Are you going away right now?" Zack can feel the emotion. He remembers how he fought back tears.

His father keeps looking around, as if confused. "I don't know. I guess so. Zack?"

Zack meets his father's eyes, trembling. They're best friends. They have a secret handshake.

"If I go away tonight, Zack. Would you . . . come with me?"

Zack glances briefly at his sleeping brother. "Yes." He knows what this is without being told. This is a dangerous thing. Like being outlaws.

"We'd have to sort of . . . hide. You wouldn't see Mommy ever again maybe."

"I don't care," and he doesn't. He loves Daddy, not Mommy. Mommy only loves the baby.

"We might get in trouble," Dad says, as if hoping Zack will talk him out of it. "But . . . the thing is . . . I feel like I just can't . . . leave you." And here is where his father cries. He doesn't wail like Josh or sniffle like Zack, or even shed tears. Something just happens inside his face. But Zack knows it is still crying.

Zack touches his father's arm. "I don't care how bad it is. Let's go."

The sun is getting hot on the soccer field. The keynote speaker is up. Cecil Cardew, the developer who built the Flamingo Mall. "Ladies and gentlemen," he says. "I believe in dreams."

They pack things in Zack's suitcase, and Zack puts on a windbreaker because it might get cold. Daddy stares at Joshua for a long time before they go.

Then they are driving, and this part is confusing because Zack sleeps on and off. He loves to ride with Dad because he drives so fast. Sometimes Zack wakes up and sees the dark trees whipping past the car. And the stars. It makes him think. "Why do trees go past the car and not the stars?"

His father, who is more distracted than usual, takes a moment to understand the question. "Because the stars are far away. When something is real far away, it doesn't look like it's moving."

Zack snuggles into his jacket. He doesn't think that makes any sense, but he appreciates his father's attempt at least to make something up, to give him an answer.

They drive all night, and then Dad needs to sleep, so they go to a Motel 6. Dad buys them waffles, and then he sleeps on the Motel 6 bed while Zack watches TV. He

118

finds a great show where women on roller skates try to knock one another down.

Dad wakes up around noon, and they eat really good cheeseburgers, the kind where the cheese melts down into the meat, and then they hit the road again. That's what Dad says. "Ready to hit the road?"

"Where are we going?" Zack asks.

His father shrugs. "It doesn't matter." And then, for no reason at all, he laughs. "It doesn't matter!" he repeats in awe.

They stop for gas. Zack loves to smell gasoline. He tries to hang out the driver's window to smell it better. "Hey!" says his father. "Straighten up and fly right." He says that a lot.

In the afternoon a mood of euphoria takes hold. It is a gorgeous October day, cool and crisp, the air scented with burning leaves, the sky a crayon-blue. Dad takes back roads so he can speed. He drives too fast. He rolls all the windows down, letting in the wind, and Zack feels like they're flying. He hangs his head out the window a little, testing the waters. Dad immediately taps his shoulder. "Hey," he says.

Zack pulls in. "What does that say?" he asks, pointing to the passenger mirror.

"Objects in the mirror are closer than they appear."

"What does that mean?"

"Well . . ." His father is looking for a cigarette. "Just like it says." He turns on the radio. The Eagles are singing "Take It to the Limit."

119

"Your wish is my command." Dad chuckles and floors it. The wind screams through the car. "Yes, Jesus!" Dad crows. He tosses his cigarette out the window and turns off the car radio. "Ready for our duet?" he asks Zack. "We have to prepare for Carnegie Hall."

"Okay." Zack loves their duet.

They sing "I Won't Grow Up" as they sail past rows and rows of apple orchards. It almost hurts Zack's eyes to see the rows flash past. One of the orchards has a fruit stand. They stop to buy a basket of apples. Dad loves apples. The fruit people let Zack climb a tree while they chat with his father. Sitting up in that tree, eating an apple and watching his dad talk to the fruit people, with the sun going down and the air turning gold . . . it might have been the happiest moment in Zack's life.

The speeches are over. The sun is hot. The new graduates rise as they did in rehearsal, and Zack rises with them, pouring sweat, shaking like a drug addict. They move two by two. Clara is near the head of the line. She takes her diploma and smiles back at Zack, and he means to smile but can't. All he can do is trudge along, while inside his mind things are jumping around crazily. It's like just before an earthquake. That rumble just before the ground breaks open.

His turn comes and he hears his name over the microphone. He manages to hold out his hand but drops the diploma and has to pick it up. It's so hot to be outside and all in black. It takes so long to read out the names of the entire class.

Last week Mr. Hirschhorn told them about the custom of throwing mortarboards into the air, and the kids all wanted to do it. As the last students file over, their classmates are stamping around like impatient cattle, waiting for the only fun part of this dreary ceremony. Then Mr. Hirschhorn gives his signal. "Ladies and gentlemen, I give you the class of—" And he is drowned out by screams, and hats go flying. Zack stands paralyzed, and some other kid takes his hat off and throws it for him.

Then he is plowing through an onrushing crowd of parents, looking for Mom and Josh, and Clara jumps him like a puppy and gives him a kiss he doesn't feel. "Call me, tonight, okay?" Okay. Although he knows he won't. There will be an earthquake between now and then. Who knows what will happen?

Clara scampers off to her parents and then there is Mom in her beautiful blue dress. She . . .

"Mom?" he says, as if unsure.

She hugs him. "Oh, you were wonderful! I'm so proud." She lets go and snaps a series of pictures.

"Don't." He puts up his hand as if she held a gun.

"You looked like an asshole the whole time," Josh says, and then Mom starts yelling at him for saying that word, and Zack just leads them silently to the car. It is so hot.

They don't even notice anything's wrong until Mom says, "Well, did we decide on Chili's?"

Zack stares at her. Who is she? He realizes he is breathing hard. "I'm not hungry."

She glances over. "Are you all right?"

"It's the heat," he says. "Can we go home?"

"Well, of course, dear. Maybe you should lie down and we'll just go out later."

"No," he says in a leaden voice. "We have to talk."

She looks over again, this time it's not just a glance. "Why? What's the matter?"

His breathing is shallow. His chest heaves. Joshua leans forward, visibly scared. Zack looks to his mother in a kind of blind desperation. "What did you do to him?" he cries. "Where is he?"

She becomes frantic now, trying to look at Zack and the road at the same time. "Where is who?"

He breaks down in horrible sobs. "My daddy!"

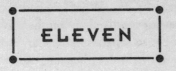

ELEVEN

Zachary really believes everything will be all right, until Dad buys the six-pack. He knows it is always a bad sign, especially bad if that is the only purpose of the errand. If Daddy had stopped for gas, for instance, and bought a whole bag of things—cigarettes, doughnuts, *and* a six-pack—that might have been okay. But he just exits the highway, drives to the nearest 7-Eleven, leaves the car without a word, returns without a word, shoves the beer behind his seat, and speeds off like a thief. Zachary wants to say something, wants to point out that beer never does anything except bring out that bad part of Daddy's personality, but he can't make himself do it. No one else is on Dad's side but him. Maybe it will be okay.

But already things are getting worse. Daddy is arguing with himself as he drives along. "It's only fair, isn't it?" he asks Zack, and Zack knows he doesn't need to answer. "Each of us gets one kid. That's the fair way." He looks at Zack pleadingly. "That's not how the courts would decide it, though. Is that what you think the courts would do?"

Zack shrugs.

"Not on your life. They'd say it was wrong to separate brothers, and they'd give you both to her. I know. I watch

123

Divorce Court every day. What's so bad about separating brothers? I never even liked *my* brother. Why don't they think it's terrible to separate fathers and sons? You know why? Because they think fathers are expendable."

"What's that?" Zack asks.

"It means they think you can just throw them away!"

Zachary gasps a little. That can't be true. Maybe this is one of Dad's exaggerations.

"If the only way to have justice is to break the law, then a person just has to break the law. Right?"

"I don't know," Zachary says.

"Look at Thoreau. Look at Dostoyevski."

"Where?" Zack looks out the window.

"Isn't it me you want to be with?" Dad asks passionately.

"Yes." That much he knows even if he isn't following the rest of this.

His father drives in silence for a minute, breathing hard. "Is that the truth, Zack? Really? Not just because you're stuck with me in the middle of nowhere. Because if you want to be with Mom and Josh, I'll take you straight home."

"And you'd go away?"

"I have to go away. That's a given."

Zachary gives it thought. Dad likes it when he thinks carefully and gives his honest opinion. "I can't talk to Mom like I can talk to you," he says.

His father exhales deeply. "That's what I thought."

Zachary keeps glancing at that six-pack in the back of the car, glittering like a snake in the sun.

•

This night they choose a Howard Johnson. Dad shows Zachary where they are on the map. Fort Wayne, Indiana. "Maybe since we're going west, we'll Go West," Dad says. The map seems to excite him. "You want to live in Colorado? Or Wyoming? And be cowboys?"

"Would I get a horse?" Zack asks.

"Sure. Why not?"

Zack is elated. Back at home they were still arguing about whether he was responsible enough to have a puppy. "Could it be a black horse with a white star on his nose?"

"Sure, sure." But Dad's smile is fading a little. He looks at the map again.

"I would name him Thunder and he'd be the fastest horse in Colorado, wouldn't he?"

Dad folds the map wrong-side out. "Let's eat dinner."

They order pizza, but only Zack eats. Dad is having a six-pack for dinner. At first it was fun because Zack went down the hall to fill an ice bucket and ice a Coke and a beer for them. But by the third beer Dad stops icing them and just drinks them warm. And Zack can see him sinking into that horrible sad mood he has seen before. He wants to shout at his father to stop drinking something that makes him sad, but understands that he can't yell at his own father.

"What's the matter with me?" Dad moans. "Am I crazy?"

Zack doesn't answer. He just chews his pizza and watches his father warily.

"Did I really think I could get away with this?" he asks. "I should be locked up."

Zack is losing his appetite. His chest feels like concrete. "Daddy . . ."

The fourth can pops open. "I am such a worthless idiot. No wonder she—"

"Daddy!"

"What?"

"Do you want an apple?" They still have some left from the orchard. Zack thinks it might help. Dad loves apples.

But somehow it's the wrong question. His father almost . . . explodes. He cries and cries, and Zachary runs to him and holds him until he's quiet.

"What's wrong?" Zack whispers.

Suddenly his father is sober again, standing up and shaking Zachary off, clearing up the empties, compressing the pizza box. "I have to take you home tomorrow," he says.

"No!"

"Yes." He is firm now, all business. Like those fathers on TV. "I have to. I'm sorry. This is wrong. I'm sorry."

"I don't want to go home!" Zachary cries.

"I know," Dad says grimly. "But it doesn't matter what we want."

126

•

Zack can't remember the drive home, but he is pretty sure they were both quiet. A few miles out of Dayton they stop at a pay phone, and Dad calls Mom and talks in a very low voice so Zachary can't hear. "Is she mad?" Zack asks when Dad comes back to the car. But he gets no answer.

Then, as they round the corner onto their street, that's when everything in the whole world goes crazy.

The street, the yard, and the driveway are full of police cars. Some of the neighbors have come out in their yards to see what it's all about. "Oh, Jesus," Dad says.

"What's going on?" Zack asks.

"It's okay," Dad says, looking terrified. "It's going to be okay."

But it's not. As soon as he puts the car in park, policemen jerk open the car doors and haul them both out. An officer lifts Zack and carries him to the porch where his mother stands. She wears a green flowered dress and looks so cold and angry, Zack breaks into a sweat. The policeman sets him down, and Mom kneels and grabs him so hard, her fingers bruise his arms. "How could you do such a thing?" she asks.

Instead of answering, Zack turns his head to see what's happening to his father. It's horrible. They have him up against the car, bent over, and they are feeling up and down his legs. "Mary, for God's sake, is this necessary?" Dad shouts over his shoulder.

She lets go of Zack and stands up. "You brought this on yourself!" she shouts back triumphantly.

"What are they doing to him?" Zack says.

She turns on him, not friendly. "You get in that house immediately, young man! I'll deal with you in a minute!"

"What are they going to do to him?" Zack shouts.

Swiftly she takes him by the collar and turns him around. Her other hand smacks his ass. The blow is harder than anything he has ever felt in his life. The impact nearly knocks him off his feet. "I told you to get in that house!" she screams.

He stumbles through the door, blinded by tears. He runs to his bedroom, where he can see out the window.

By the time he gets there, Dad has gone crazy, twisting up out of the officers' grip to face his wife. "You leave that boy alone!" he shouts at Mom. "This isn't his fault!"

Just like Zack, he is punished for his outburst. The police are all over him, four of them now instead of two. They twist his arms behind his back and slam his face into the hood of the car, kicking his legs apart with their feet. Then they handcuff him and drag him, kicking and screaming, to one of the police cruisers. Dad is almost crying now. He shouts, "It's not fair!" as they shove and stuff him into the back of the cruiser. They drive away, and then the other officers get into their cars and drive away. Finally the neighbors drift back into their houses.

Slowly Zack becomes aware of Josh, who is sitting up in bed and crying steadily. Zack is still sore from his smack.

She did it in front of all those people. And that's nothing. She called those policemen to come and beat up his father and chain him and take him away. Zack feels a cold, gripping fear. It's true. Dad wasn't exaggerating at all. Fathers *are* expendable.

She is coming now. He hears the front door close. He hears her coming down the hall. She is really angry and there's no telling what she'll do. Now he knows what she's capable of.

The bedroom door opens. Zack edges back from the window, keeping his hands behind him, trying to back into the shadows in the corner of the room. But she doesn't even look at him. She goes straight to Josh. She picks him up, rocks him and kisses him. She doesn't even look in Zack's direction. When Josh stops crying, she puts him gently on his bed and leaves the room without a word.

Zack stumbles to his bed and pulls himself up on his stomach. He is too shaken even to cry. He sees how it is. She thinks he's a traitor for going with Daddy. She will never forgive him for this. And when she gets angry with people . . . she throws them away.

Zack knows what he has to do. He will have to work hard, very hard, to make her forget this. He won't ask any questions about Daddy. He can't risk it. The only way to survive now is to pretend that none of this ever happened.

•

The ride home is very quiet except for Zack's snuffling. He calms down, but really hates himself for that outburst. It has weakened his position, made it impossible to question her from an attitude of righteous anger, as he had hoped.

He is astonished at her driving calmly home as if the whole world hadn't shattered. He is astonished at Josh's indifference. His brother looks out the car window instead of demanding to know what this is all about. Maybe they don't understand. Maybe they just think he has gone crazy.

They pull into the driveway. Josh gets out of the car and goes straight into the house. Mom fools around in the car, gathering up Zack's cap and gown and her folded program. He stands behind her, marveling at her cool. "We're going to talk about this!" he warns.

She straightens up, looks at him blandly. "We can talk about anything you want." And she walks past him into the house.

For a minute Zack just stands there watching the heat shimmer on the driveway. Maybe he is crazy. Maybe this never happened. Maybe they are in there right now whispering together and phoning 911. He wishes he could just walk away from the house, just leave and start over. But he doesn't want to let her win, so he squares his shoulders and goes inside.

They are in the kitchen making ice cube noises, like now it's time to have a cocktail party. Unbelievable. Beamer rushes up and puts his forepaws on Zack's shoulders. "You want to go out?" Zack asks. He leads the dog through the kitchen to the back door.

"Do you want a Coke?" Joshua asks in a careful voice. He does think Zack is crazy.

Zack opens the door and watches wistfully as Beamer charges into the yard and romps around. "No, I don't. I want to go into the living room and talk."

Mrs. Lloyd picks up her Coke and walks out of the kitchen.

Josh immediately turns on Zack. "What the hell is this? What are you trying to do?" he whispers. "Today of all days!"

"This is important," Zack tells him.

"Yeah, sure. Everything about *you* is always important, isn't it?" He exits.

Someday you'll thank me, Zack thinks, *you stupid son of a bitch.*

He enters the hostile living room. The only sound is that of ice cubes shifting as they sip, nearly in unison. Zack perches on the edge of a chair. He decides to open with the heavy ammunition. "Dad's not dead, is he?"

Joshua gasps. The sipping comes to an abrupt halt. Mom sets her glass on the carpet, screwing it into the pile so it won't tip. "No. He's not."

Zack holds her eyes, anger making him steady. "All these years you've been lying to us."

She looks pretty steady herself. "I had to."

"Why?"

Her face is composed, but she's breathing hard. "When

you're a mother, you do whatever you have to to protect your children."

Zack can't speak for a minute. He is too angry. He looks at Josh who is hugging himself and visibly trembling. For his sake, Zack knows he has to go on with this. "Where is he?"

"In South Carolina."

"You know his address?" Zack's heart pounds.

"Yes. He pays child support."

"Mom!" Josh explodes. "Are you just humoring him? Or what? This isn't really *true*, is it?"

She looks at him. "It's true. I didn't want you boys to ever know what kind of a man you had for a father. I thought it was better to have a nice memory of a dead man than to know the truth about that person."

"You stop it!" Zack jumps up. "That's not true! He was a nice man! I remember him!"

"Obviously," she says, "there are some things you don't remember."

"I remember you siccing the cops on him and you let them beat him up and put handcuffs on him and stuff him in a police car!"

"Do you remember that he tried to kidnap you?"

"It wasn't kidnapping! He—we ran away together!"

She shakes her head sadly. "Oh, Zachary."

"You . . . What happened after they took him away?"

Josh has gone white and rigid. He seems on the verge of having some kind of fit.

Mrs. Lloyd plucks at her skirt. "I let him cool his heels

132

in jail for a while and then I filed criminal charges against him, and to avoid *prison*, he let himself be declared unfit and I got a court order to keep him away from you boys forever." She actually smiles.

Zack feels cold. "You hate him, don't you?"

She takes a deep breath. "I don't hate anyone, Zachary. But he was never a good father and I couldn't let him get away with child abuse."

"He didn't abuse me!"

Suddenly her voice lifts to a roar. "He *kidnapped* you!"

"How can you call it kidnapping? If you had run off and taken me somewhere . . ."

"First, I wouldn't do that. I would have no reason to. He did it because I was finally serious about divorcing him and he knew he wouldn't have a snowball's chance in hell of getting custody with all his lovely habits. So, in his typical way, he tried to make his own rules. Well, not this time. Not when it comes to separating a mother from her children. That was something he didn't understand. He could get away with a lot around me, but he shouldn't have tried to interfere with my rights as a mother."

"What about his rights as a father?"

Suddenly she stands up. Her calmness has hardened into a cold fury. She looks just like she did that day, when she smacked him and made him go into the house. "He is indeed your biological father, Zachary. There is nothing I can do about that. But let me just clarify a few points for you. This man was completely selfish and irresponsible. He didn't want to get a decent job; he drank constantly and made a fool of himself at every opportunity. He treated me like dirt. He was thoughtless, neglectful, and childish. When I finally decided I couldn't take any more, he viciously . . ." She pauses for breath. ". . . viciously thought of the one way to take revenge that would hurt me the most. He took my son; he took my own *child* and left without a word. You were gone two days. I nearly went *insane*. Did he care? Of course not. He never thought of anyone but himself. Then, I suppose, when he realized that he'd have to actually be responsible for you and have to take care of you, he just phoned and said he wanted to come back. Well, I apologize if you think I was harsh, but I didn't think he should get away scot-free with a stunt like that. Foolishness is one thing, but endangering a *child* is something else. What he did was a crime. He was very lucky I didn't tell them to lock him up and throw away the key. Now, you tell me what you think I did wrong. Do you think I was wrong to get an injunction? Should I have to go around worrying he might come back to steal you again? I'm sorry. No, I didn't tell you boys the truth because I thought it was too frightening for little children. I wanted you to have a calm, safe home to grow up in. You didn't seem to remember anything, and I thought that was a blessing. I didn't want you to remember being kidnapped by a drunken lunatic. I knew all along that this therapy would only hurt you. Ever since you started, you've done nothing but lash out at me. Well, fine. I can take it. It goes with the territory. And if you want to make some kind of speech to me about my deceiving you, you'd better stop and think first. Which one of your parents really cared about you, Zack? All I ever tried to do was protect you and help you. I've been here all along taking care of you. And the man you seem to want to defend just used you. He made you into some kind of horrible tool in his fight with me. And if you think there's something *glamorous* about that, then there's nothing else I can say. Excuse me."

Zack and Josh watch her go down the hall to her room and shut the door. Then they look at each other. The house is very quiet. The ice cubes in Mom's glass shift, and both boys jump.

Zack feels the need to defend himself. "She *lied*," he says lamely.

Josh shakes himself, as if trying to wake up. "I don't want to talk about any of this right now," he says in a rather high voice. "This is a lot to take in at once."

"But . . ."

Josh stands. "I mean it!" And he goes down the hall too. Another door closes.

Slowly Zachary gets up. He gathers their dirty glasses, rinses them, and puts them in the dishwasher. The house is completely silent. He opens the back door and wanders into the yard. The heat is overwhelming. Beamer shuffles toward him, then slows down, sensing Zack's state of mind. He stops a few respectful feet away and cocks his head.

Zack sits on the grass. He doesn't feel any emotions. His mind is like a drawer that has been pulled out and turned upside down, emptied of all its contents except two little words, which are stuck there somehow and keep repeating themselves to him.

South Carolina.

TWELVE

Clara's father answers the door; scowls when he sees who it is. "Clara's busy now," he says, propping a muscular arm across the doorway. "We're having her graduation party."

In the living room a rabble of voices are laughing, bullying, calling to one another. Farther away, in the kitchen, there is a melodious racket of cooking—clang, slam, clink—punctuated by feminine giggling. Zack knows nothing about family gatherings, since his whole family is stranded back in Ohio.

"Just for a second?" he asks. "It's kind of an emergency."

Mr. Benedetto gives a cold stare to this boy who has an "emergency" to discuss with his daughter. "Aw, Christ!" he says, and closes the door.

Zack isn't sure if this is acquiescence or dismissal. He waits it out in the blazing sun.

When the door opens again, it's his girl in a pink and white striped sundress; her earrings look like pieces of candy. Zack, who feels low on love and acceptance, longs to grab her and crush her against him, but there's no point in starting a war with Italy. "Hi," he says nervously.

She looks puzzled, slightly irritated. "Hi," she says. "Did you forget my family was coming over? I told you I'd call you tonight."

He shifts his weight. He is perspiring. "I know. But something sort of . . . funny came up. Can you talk for a minute?"

She doesn't look pleased at all. "What is it? My whole family's here. Can't it wait?"

"Just come for a drive with me," he says, and hears the pleading in his voice. "Just a half hour. I need somebody to talk to."

Her eyes are getting colder rather than warmer. "We're going to eat dinner in a little while."

He feels a rush of desperation, as if somehow he must make her do this or he will die. "Please!" he wails.

The babble in the living room stops dead. Everyone is listening. Zack feels his face go hot. "Oh, look, never mind!" He turns to leave.

She catches his arm. "Just a minute. Stay there." Like her dad, she closes the door.

While he waits, the sun is almost unbearable. A troop of ants starts climbing over his tennis shoe. He stomps them, crushing and smearing their bodies on the concrete. A sob of self-pity rises in his throat, and it takes everything he's got to fight it back down.

Clara returns; her expression is not friendly. But she does come outside, closing the door behind her. "This is just great," she says. "Now my whole family is going to think I'm pregnant." She starts off across the lawn, past

138

the driveway and sidewalk full of cars, hunting for Zack's Toyota.

He trails behind. "Why would anybody think that?"

"You wouldn't understand." She locates the car and jerks impatiently on the locked passenger door. Zack hurries to get in and open it for her. She drops into the passenger seat, her skirt settling in a pouf around her legs.

Zack smells lilacs. He looks hungrily at her bare legs. She has a little scratch on her right knee. For a minute he feels he doesn't really want to talk at all. He just wants to touch her and let her touch him. It would be so comforting right now, he thinks, with the whole world gone crazy, to just get lost in all that starchy cotton and female warmth and forget everything else.

He turns on the air, watching it lift the curls on her forehead. "Do you want to drive around or just talk here?" he asks.

"Drive a few blocks away, anyway!" she snaps, flouncing about as if his seats were uncomfortable. "My cousins are probably watching this whole thing with binoculars."

"Okay." He starts the ignition with a trembling hand.

"And look. This better not take long. I said I'd be back in a half hour."

Her anger and impatience make him feel as if he can't breathe. But he tells himself it will be okay. When she finds out what this is about, she'll be sorry she was so rude.

He drives to a minipark near a canal, so they have something pretty to look at. He kills the engine and switches to the battery so they can have air. A white heron breaks from the trees and flaps slowly across the water. "Look!" Zack says.

She turns on him. "Zack, for Pete's sake, what do you want?"

He runs his hands over his face and up through his hair. "Okay. You know about my nightmares and everything? Well, I found out what they mean. I was right. I've been repressing memories of my father. My therapist—"

She clamps a hand on his knee. "Whoa. Your *what*?"

"Nancy. My therapist. She—"

"You're in *analysis*?" She looks as if he had just confessed to adultery.

"I've been getting counseling," he says. "Because of my dreams. Nancy told me they might be repressed memories and—"

"Why didn't you tell me this before?" She has raised her voice. Her eyes are blazing.

"Didn't I? I thought I did."

"This is just great!" she says. "Just what I need."

He's angry now. It's hard enough to tell this and she's messing up his concentration. "What do you mean just what *you* need?" he shouts. "This is about *me*! Clara, you knew all this. I told you my dreams might be about my father. You even gave me that tiger poem!"

"I knew you were having the dreams and everything. That's what I knew. I sure as hell didn't know you were going to a shrink!"

"Nancy's not a psychiatrist!" he yells. "She's a psychologist. There's a difference."

"There's not that much difference! They're both for people who can't cope with their problems!"

Zack folds his arms. He's shaking and sweating with anger. "Well, that's just ignorant!"

"It's not! I know all about it, unfortunately. I know that people like you who want to sit and suck your thumb all day and whimper about your childhood just end up . . . *nowhere*!" With the last word she actually puts her hands up and shoves his shoulders, like a little kid asking for a fight. Then she suddenly turns her face away, turns her whole back to him. She sniffles and Zack realizes she's crying.

Finally he comes to see they aren't really talking about him. Or at least she isn't. "Clara?" he says.

She sniffs again. He opens the glove compartment and takes out a pack of tissues, offering them to her. "Thank you," she says in a broken voice.

He puts a tentative hand between her shoulder blades. She flinches but doesn't pull away. "What is all this?" he asks.

She is busy blowing her nose, not the most attractive thing he has ever seen her do. "I'm sorry, Zack." Her voice sounds flat and exhausted. "You just took me by surprise, you know?"

"Oh, come on. It's more than that. Have you had counseling or something?"

She shakes her head. "Thank God, no. But . . ." She

looks at him suddenly, turns and gazes at him with pure longing. She wants to tell something. Zack remembers then that she has a secret too.

"Is this about that bridge?" he asks.

She just stares, as if she hadn't heard. Then a sort of shudder goes through her. "I can't talk about it."

Zack has pretty well forgotten his own trauma for the moment. "Yes you can. You tell me yours and I'll tell you mine."

She laughs, dabbing at her eyes. "And then we can drive straight into the canal."

Zack doesn't answer this. It's a little too scary to be funny. "Tell me about the bridge," he says quietly.

She pulls down the sun visor to check her makeup for tear damage. Then she takes a couple of deep breaths. "Back in New Jersey," she says, "I got mixed up with this boy. Danny Gemmelli. We . . ." She hesitates, looking at Zack warily. "We got very close . . . you know?"

"Yeah, okay!" Zack waves his hand. "He was the one you—"

"That's right. I thought I was really in love with him. He was sort of shy, quiet. The sensitive type. Oh, God. That's what I thought I wanted. Most of the boys in my neighborhood were like animals, you know? No, you don't know. It seemed like they were all bastards. Not like you Kansas types." She labeled everything that was not New York or New Jersey as "Kansas." "Just for an example. Once when I was thirteen a bunch of boys from my class started following me when I was walking home from school, and they grabbed me and dragged me in an alley and took my panties off. You know, just held me and pulled them off. That was their idea of a prank. I guess I'm supposed to be glad that was all they did, but it's a hell of a way to get to know boys. I was all set to be a nun, I'm not kidding. I thought, if I had to marry anybody from that pig gender, the hell with it."

Zack tries to concentrate, although part of his mind is hung up on the idea of tracking these boys down and cutting their throats.

She pauses to blow her nose again. "So anyway, my sophomore year I met Danny. Don't be jealous, Zack, but he was beautiful. Sort of slender, maybe you'd even say delicate, but not in a feminine way. Like . . . graceful. Brown eyes, dark hair—"

"Okay, okay. I don't need his measurements."

"I'm trying to explain how I felt, so this will make sense. The other girls didn't go for Danny, you know? Because he wore glasses and he was shy. In my school a guy was macho or dead. And there was Danny, always sitting by himself, reading a book."

"A regular Lord Byron!" Zack says. "I'm sorry. I'll shut up."

"Thank you. So I started hanging around him, talking to him. He was brilliant and just . . . really sweet and considerate. It was like somebody had left a jewel in the mud and I was the one who found it and polished it up. We started dating and we were really good for each other. I sort of drew him out and gave him confidence. He gave me books to read, made me think about things. And over the summer we fell in love."

"Okay!" Zack holds up his hand. "I'm listening but don't go into the details about—"

"I wasn't going to. But that happened over the summer, and, well, you know, when that happens you . . . feel close. But then something went wrong."

Zack catches his breath, terrified there is a pregnancy coming in this story.

Clara has paused as if this part of the account confuses her. "Something went wrong between us. I guess it was my fault. Because suddenly . . . I don't know, I felt crowded. At the end of every date Danny would have to make the next date, like he thought I would try to escape. He called me every day, and when I had to hang up, he would keep on talking. He started talking about marriage! Then he took all his money, his whole college fund, and bought me a diamond. It was too much! I was only seventeen. I mean, he was sweet, but he wasn't . . . Well, I didn't know it at the time, but he wasn't *you*. He wasn't somebody I could go on with forever."

Zack's breathing quickens as he realizes the declaration she's just made to him. He doesn't think she herself realizes it, because she goes right on. "I refused the ring and we had a huge fight. Well, it wasn't a fight because Danny didn't operate like that. He cried and said he couldn't go on. He could feel me pulling away and it was killing him . . . and I couldn't say much because it was true. I felt like . . . almost like he was some kind of quicksand pulling me down. I was panicked. I told him we should see other people. And that was the last real conversation we had."

There is something so cold and final in her tone, Zack suddenly realizes with horror where this story is going. Her painting of the bridge looms in his mind, and he understands now what he has always seen in the picture; the finality of a scaffold or a guillotine. A towering, steel tombstone.

"He went into analysis. That's why I went crazy a second ago. When I think of analysis, I think of Danny. And it didn't help him. He kept unraveling, further and further. He sent me all these crazy notes, these horrible notes where he accused me of being cruel and destroying his life, and I ignored them because I thought that was the right thing to do. I thought he should face reality. And then I got this long, like thirteen-page letter . . ." She breaks off and covers her face with her hands.

"Suicide note," Zack says quietly.

She nods. Her shoulders convulse. Zack pulls her into his arms. He kisses her hair. She clings to him and cries. He has never felt so close to another human being in his life. And he aches for the same release she is feeling. In a minute he'll be telling her his story, and maybe he'll want to cry, too, and she'll hold him just like this.

She sobs, letting it all out. When she is completely spent, she sits up and heartily attacks the tissues again. "The police found his car parked on the bridge. I had to be a part of the whole investigation. I had to go and make a statement and they took my letter and passed it around, and then it got into the media. Parts of this letter, really personal stuff on the six o'clock news. And my name, all those newspeople saying my name. Like the cause of death. Can you imagine? That was why we moved down here. It was hard on Dad. It was hard on *me*. My parents were almost like ashamed of me, I guess. I don't know. So we moved."

Zack embraces her again. "Oh, sweetheart," he says. "None of it was your fault."

She pulls away and looks at her watch. "God. They'll kill me."

"The hell with them. You needed to talk. And I do too. See, these memories were pushing through and then I remembered some weird stuff about my mom and dad. They sort of . . . broke up and she tried to kick him out and he . . . he and I ran away together for two days."

She looks up, surprised. "Really? When was this? I mean how old were you?"

"Five."

"And your dad actually abducted you?"

"No! I went with him!"

She purses her lips. "Zachary. No five-year-old would leave his mother voluntarily."

"I did! I liked him better. I loved my father."

"He must have threatened you or scared you or something."

"No, you don't understand! My father was . . . special. Anyway, after two days he realized he couldn't really

146

get away with it. So he brought me home. But Mom had called the police and they were all over and she pressed charges and I watched them take him away!"

She brushes her hand over his leg. "Oh, Zachary. So when he died, you felt bad because you wished you'd run away and had that time with him?"

"No." He still trembles with this new information. "He didn't die."

"Huh?"

Zack feels a swell of pure joy. "My father isn't dead."

"But I thought . . ."

"My mother lied to me. To us. She kept him away with a court order. And she told us he was dead."

"Are you serious?"

"Yes. I remembered most of it this morning and I made Mom tell me the rest. My father . . ." He pauses to shiver. ". . . lives in South Carolina."

"Wow."

Zachary is ready now for the final release, the showing of emotions. Just as Clara had done. "All my life," he says, "I've never had a single fight with my mom. Do you know why? I mean, I need to discuss this with Nancy, but I think it's because I'm *scared* of Mom. I think when I was a little boy, I got the idea she was ruthless because of what she did to Dad. I thought, if you pissed her off, she could just call the cops and have you taken away! I thought she might do that to me. I was . . . like muzzled. That's why I forgot everything. Because I was scared. I've always felt guilty around her, like she doesn't love me as much as Josh. See why? Because I betrayed her to go with Dad. When I think about it . . ." He pauses to gather and feel his own anger. ". . . what she did was *despicable*! She let those cops beat my father up right in front of me! She deprived me of my father the whole time I was growing up just to be vindictive! She lied to me about my own life! All these years she's just . . . *lied*! I always felt she was so good and perfect and I was so bad. And all this time she was deliberately hurting me and my father, keeping us apart. Well, she's not going to do it anymore! You know what I'm going to do? I'm going to find out where he is and go to him!" He hadn't known until this second that he was planning any such thing, but it is obvious. He has to do it. Zack feels wonderful, triumphant, purged. He looks at Clara.

She is just staring at the dashboard. "Wow," she says. She looks at her watch again.

Zack feels guilty for taking so much time. He had promised not to get her in trouble. "You need to get back, don't you?"

She lifts her eyes to his, in an expression he can't quite read. "Yeah, I really do."

Something is wrong. Zack feels he should have gotten more than this, a hug at the very least. "I didn't mean I was going to South Carolina to *stay*," he says. "But I want to see him and talk to him. I have a right."

"Yes, you do," she says, reaching for the seat belt. "I've really got to go."

He stops her hand. "What's wrong?"

"Nothing!"

"Something is!"

She exhales with exasperation. "Zack! I'm really late! We haven't got time to go into it now!"

"Go into what? What did I say?"

"This is just a lot to take in."

"How do you think *I* feel?"

"I can't imagine. And . . . look, you've been through a big thing. You're confused. Let's just not talk about it for a few days."

"What are you telling me? Stay away from you until I get everything straight?"

"That might be a good idea." She is looking away.

Zack, who is hardly ever angry, feels his rage boil over for a second time that day. "I get it," he says, shoving the emergency brake. "You don't want to run any risk I'll go bats like good old sweet sensitive Danny, right?"

Her mouth is tight. "I didn't say that."

He wants to slap her. He wants to make a fist and *slug* her. He jerks the gearshift and fires the engine and shifts again, flooring it, so they lurch backward and swing around crazily. Clara scrambles for her seat belt.

Good! he thinks. *Boo! Be scared, you bitch!* "You're just priceless," he hisses as he merges recklessly with traffic. "You want a guy with a warranty, don't you? I guess you think I might turn out to be another jumper!"

"Stop it," she says.

"You stop it!" he shouts back. "I thought we were close! I thought we were friends! I thought you were the one person who could understand this! When you told your damn story I *cared*, Clara. I felt for you. But when you heard mine, all you could think was, Damaged goods. Right?"

"That's not fair," she murmurs.

They are already at her house. He turns in at a bad angle and slams the brakes, pitching her forward. "Get out!" he growls.

She turns to him tearfully. "You don't understand! After all I've been through . . . the reason I liked you in the first place was because you seemed so calm and . . . stable! Like nothing ever bothered you. I thought that would be so comforting!"

He reaches across her and shoves her door open. "Surprise!" he says bitterly. "I'm a human being like everyone else!"

She tries to hesitate and he actually pushes her. Blinded by tears, she stumbles up on the curb.

"You don't want a boyfriend!" he screams as he guns the engine. "You want a houseplant!" He roars away hoping the cousins heard everything.

THIRTEEN

Zack opens his eyes hopefully, but the world is still there. Worse than that, it's summer, Zack's least favorite season. The time when Florida, which he dislikes anyway, goes from mildly irritating to unbearable. When the heat clings like a damp blanket. When ants go insane and invade homes and shoes. When he has to find a job, probably in some cholesterol pit. When every afternoon erupts into a thunderstorm of volcanic intensity. When hurricanes form and tease all the coastal cities with destruction. That's all. And no school. Now Zack is stuck in the house for three months with a mother and a brother who are politely shunning him for having the gall to reclaim his own memories. And his psychologist has gone west for two weeks with her husband and children, leaving Zack a drippy message on her answering machine. If he has an "emergency," he should call her colleague Harvey Roothandler, as if Zack would trust his psyche to a man with a name like that. And he has lost his best friend and his lover all at once, since Clara doesn't mess with people like Zack who are potentially crazy. That's all. Now why would a few simple setbacks like that ruin a guy's summer?

Zack shifts in bed and turns to see the only comforting thing left in his world. There's Beamer, waiting patiently for him to wake up, tongue flopping out over a big, silly dog-grin, body heaving up and down with happy, heavy dog-breathing. Beamer doesn't care if there are cross-currents in the house. He couldn't care less if his best friend is crazy. All he wants is a morning hug. And he gets it.

"Oh, Sunbeam," Zack says, pulling handfuls of blond fur toward his face, breathing in warm animal-smell.

Beamer stumbles from this unexpected display of affection, but then joins in eagerly, pinning Zack with his forepaws and licking his face. Zack giggles, but the sound is forced. This is the worst disappointment of all. There are some kinds of pain even a dog can't cure.

Stripped of all his illusions, Zack sits up, gently pushing Beamer aside. Still happily ignorant, Sunbeam pads off to the boys' bathroom to see if there are any shower puddles worth drinking. *If only we could change places*, Zack thinks, watching the blond tail-plume disappear around the corner.

Zack gets up and puts on a robe, raking his hair into place with his fingers. Then he opens the bedroom door and walks quietly into Enemy Territory. The VCR clock says nine A.M. Good. Mom is already at work, molding other young minds. But Zack can feel Joshua in the house. Intuition guides him to the kitchen, where he finds his brother sitting at the table in just his briefs. His hair falls in his eyes as he sleepily eats Froot Loops and studies the cereal box, which promises to send him to California if he can find the forty toucans hidden in a picture of a jungle. All in all, he looks about twelve years old.

Zack announces himself warily. "Hi."

Josh jumps as if Jason, Freddy, and Michael Meyers had all walked in. His big blue eyes flick over Zack. "Hi."

"Mom go to work?"

"Yeah." Josh turns his attention back to the toucan picture.

Zack doesn't know what to do. He doesn't want a confrontation, but it might be better than being treated like furniture. He gets a bowl and takes the Froot Loops box from Josh's hand, forcing him to look up. "Is Mom mad at me?"

Josh's eyes are veiled. "Why should she be?"

"I don't know." Zack pours milk on his cereal and sits down. "Are you?"

"What."

"Mad."

"At who?"

"At me!" Zack is exhausted, and they haven't gotten anywhere.

Josh waits a long time before answering. "You haven't done anything, have you?"

Zack lifts his chin. "No, I haven't."

"Well, then . . ." Now that the box is taken away, Josh just looks down at his cereal. Zack realizes no one in his family makes good eye contact. They're like convicts.

"I couldn't help remembering what I remembered, could I?" Zack says pleadingly. He hates to humble himself this way, but Josh is the closest thing to a friend he has left.

"I don't know. No. You couldn't help it. You're right. So now you've remembered it. Let's get back to normal."

Without warning, Zack is angry. Furious. Blind with rage. "You don't care a thing about him, do you?"

"Who?"

"Our father!"

Josh pushes his cereal aside. "No! Frankly, I don't. Mom says he was a scuz-bag and that's good enough for me. She raised us. She did all the stuff. Where was he?" He looks up with his eyes flashing.

"She wouldn't let him near us! It was her doing!"

"See? That's what I don't like about all this. The way you talk about *her* now. Like she's . . . bad." Tears sparkle in Josh's eyes.

Zack softens his voice. "No, no, I don't think . . . but she . . . Didn't she do a bad thing? Isn't it bad to tell us all those lies?"

"Well, I think . . . I think it's probably real hard to raise kids by yourself and whatever she did was to protect us, and I trust her if she says he was no good and I'm glad she kept him away. So don't . . . I don't know what you're going to do now, but if you're going to try to . . . contact him or something, just please leave me out of it because I'm not going to hurt her over some guy I don't even know!" Josh gets up, shoving his chair in clumsily.

154

"And another thing! Maybe she did get that court order and everything, but where is he *now*? Did you think about that? You've been eighteen a whole year and he knows where we are! So where is he? Where's this great guy you think you remember? You're dreaming!" He stands there one more second, hovering between anger and tears, and then runs off. In a flurry of slams and bangs, he dresses and flees the house.

Eighteen or not, Zack feels he's entitled to cry, especially since there are no witnesses. He tries to put his head down on the table, but the Froot Loops are in the way; so he picks up the whole bowl and heaves it at the back door. It shatters, making a colorful, dripping mess. Zack puts his face in his hands. After a second he feels a heavy bumping at his side and realizes Beamer has come to comfort him. Another good thing about dogs. They don't ask why. You're crying, you're my friend, good enough for me. Zack buries his fingers in fur. "It's okay," he says, pulling himself together. "I'm okay. Really."

Beamer believes this and turns his attention to the back door where he sees to his delight that Zack has created a lovely moving, edible work of art. Wagging his whole body, he checks it out, licking the pastel drips and crunching Froot Loops underfoot.

Together they clean up the kitchen and then it's ten A.M. Only thirteen hot, lonely, empty hours until bedtime. Back in the bedroom, searching for clean underwear, Zack pauses in front of his painting. Now the shadow in the background is a real man, a man he knows, reaching out to him. That orchard. That beautiful orchard they visited together. But what do the tigers mean? This is still a mystery. It must be part of another memory, fused into this one.

Zack keeps staring at the hand, and the shadow behind it. Somewhere in South Carolina this shadow is walking around doing South Carolina things. Sitting on a veranda drinking lemonade or something. Why South Carolina? Lots of Ohioans go to Florida, but Zack has never heard of one going to South Carolina. Maybe he breeds race-horses or runs a cotton plantation. No, he's supposed to be a drifter, an odd-jobber. He's probably mucking out stables and *picking* cotton. But still. He has those eyes Zack can now remember. Warm, happy, coy, laughing eyes. And he sings songs from the score of *Peter Pan*. And now that he remembers him, Zack misses him.

In the shower he thinks of nothing else. He tends his new memories like a fire, coaxing out details. He pictures the roads they drove on, the floor plan of each motel where they stayed. And then another memory pops in, whole and perfect.

•

Zack is sitting on the floor of the room where Daddy works. He is about four. He plays with a pull toy, a yellow duck on wheels, which makes a noisy quacking sound.

"Jeez!" his father calls. "Go get a stuffed animal, kid! Your duck sounds like something trying to throw up in a garbage can!"

Zack laughs and looks around. Daddy is standing up to work today, not using his stool. Behind him, in a playpen, Josh snoozes and drools. Zack goes to his father and embraces his knees. "Do magic!" he says, looking up with his most charming smile, the one that gets Daddy to do everything.

"Magic!" Daddy says, kneeling down. "Again? Aren't you getting sick of magic? You've seen this magic about ten hundred million times!"

Zack pummels his father playfully. "Do it! Do it! Do it!"

Daddy laughs. It's a great sound. "Okay! Okay! Have mercy! I surrender! What color magic do you want?"

Zack likes them all, but he finally decides. "Purple."

"Okay. Purple magic it is. Let me see now, that's rather difficult . . . all right. Here we are." He takes one of his little boards from a shelf. "First we need some . . . what?"

"Blue!" Zachary shouts, hugging himself with excitement. He loves this game.

"Blue? Are you sure? Are you positive?"

Zack laughs. "Yes!"

"All right. If you say so." Dad takes a tube, just like toothpaste, and squirts out a little worm of blue. Brilliant, glorious blue. Zack stares at it because it's so pretty. "Then what?" Daddy asks.

"Red!" Zack cries.

"Red? Oh, no, that can't be. Now you've gone too far. I think we make purple with black."

"No, it's red. Do it right, Daddy!" Zack insists.

His father sighs. "Okay, but you're very bossy for a volunteer from the audience. Okay, are you ready for the magic part?" He carefully squirts out a crimson worm next to the blue one.

"Yes," Zack says breathlessly.

Daddy takes a brush from his big glass jar and holds it over the paint. "You say the magic words while I mix."

Zack chants softly, "The check . . . is in . . . the mail."

And Dad swirls the red and the blue, and at first it looks like the magic won't happen, but then it does. Purple. Swirls of purple, getting bigger and more beautiful every second.

"Oh!" Zack sighs. "That was perfect!"

His father grins at him. "You're easy. I hope you grow up to be an art critic."

•

Zack has been in the shower too long. The water is scorching the back of his neck like intense sunlight. But he can't move. His father is a painter. His father is a painter. And Mom never told him. He's a painter just like his father, and no one cared enough to tell him. It would have meant. . . . Zack turns off the water and stands there until all the drips have stopped.

He dresses slowly and deliberately, like a soldier. Or a criminal. He plans his mission in his mind. He has never entered her room without permission. She taught them both to respect privacy. There is an inflexible rule about opening other people's mail. Now, he can see the sinister side of that. Countless times, checks and letters from *him* have come to this house. Zack racks his brain, trying to think of all the hand-addressed letters he has carried to Mom from the mailbox. Has there been a recurring South Carolina postmark? Why hasn't he been more observant? He has probably touched his father's envelopes a million times. If he had lapsed just once and opened her mail, he might have known the truth. But no. He wouldn't have dreamed of doing it. He has been raised to be honorable. Well, no more. She hasn't played straight with him. Now it is war.

Still, he trembles as he crosses the threshold of her room. He feels like he's doing something dirty. She has a little desk where she pays bills and grades papers and writes to an endless stream of aunts and cousins. It's a pretty, feminine desk, gold and white, the top littered with sentimental claptrap. Such as the World's Best Mom coffee mug he gave her one Mother's Day. It mocks him now as he pulls out drawers and riffles through her papers and letters. Nothing. Maybe she destroys Dad's envelopes the minute they come.

Then he sees her address book. No. It couldn't be that simple. All these years, watching her address Christmas cards, flipping through this battered little book with the hyacinths on the cover. Surely, he couldn't have picked it up at any time and found Dad between Aunt Ruth and the dry cleaner! Could he?

Even though he has just showered, Zack is perspiring. He opens the book to the L section. And there it is.

AL
1897 Blue Heron Way
Hilton Head Island, SC 29938
(803) 555-1884

Of course, even if he had seen this, it wouldn't have meant anything to him. He wouldn't have associated "AL" with Anthony Lloyd. That was a dead man. He would never have given this entry a second look. But he gazes at it now.

Hilton Head Island. His father lives on an island. The veranda melts away and is replaced by a beach and marina. His father is wearing cutoffs and painting sailboats. He squints into the sun. Sea gulls fly over him.

Zack tries to picture his father's house on Blue Heron Way. The name sounds magical, like something from a children's book. Zack's chest aches with a longing to see Blue Heron Way. The address alone makes his father seem even more real. And since Zack has a phone number . . . His heart begins to pound . . . He could do it, right now, this morning. This minute. He could pick up his mom's French telephone and rip a corridor in time and space, straight to Blue Heron Way. And his long-dead father would come up out of the shadows and hold out his hand like God reaching to Adam in the Sistine Chapel.

And they would touch.

Zack is dizzy. He sits down at the desk, staring at the phone, listening to his own pulse beating in his head. He reaches for the receiver. Wait! She'd see this on the phone bill! Well, but who cares? Let her see it! He reaches again. He picks up the receiver and listens to five minutes of dial tone. A recording comes on and admonishes him. He holds the button down while he gets ready. What can he say? It doesn't matter. The important thing is to hear his father's voice. That lovely, mellow, tenor-sax voice he remembers. He could just let his father say hello, and hang up! This gives him courage. He dials the number fast before he can lose his nerve. It rings. It rings again.

"Hello?"

Zack is stunned, chilled, blown apart. The sound resonates in his head, in his whole body. This is his father's voice. His father is speaking to him.

"Hel*lo?*" Pissed off. About to disconnect.

"Hello?" Zack croaks. He can barely hear over the roar in his head. "Is this Anthony Lloyd?"

"You got it!" Friendly but impatient. "What can I do for you?"

Say anything! Keep him on the line! "Would you be interested in a subscription to *Popular Science* magazine?"

"No way! Have a nice day!" *Click.*

He's gone. But it was him. It was really him. Zack replaces the receiver, feeling interesting tremors up and down his arms and legs. He realizes that up until this moment he hasn't quite believed in any of it. But it's true. For the second time this morning Zack puts his head down and cries. Only this time it's for joy.

After that, everything comes easily. Zack is focused and single-minded as he packs his clothes and portfolio. He calls AAA for routing information, writes a long note to his mother and then tears it up. She doesn't deserve it. Instead, he tears the L page from her address book and leaves it on the kitchen table. That says it all.

He counts the money in his wallet. Twenty dollars. Not much, but enough.

He stuffs a backpack with provisions; a box of Chocolate Teddy Grahams, two bottles of Evian, and some apples. Beamer follows him about the kitchen, and they discuss the situation. "My father asked me to run away with him once," Zack explains. "And now I'm asking you. You want to go with me or stay here with these hypocrites?"

Beamer understands perfectly. He goes to the back door and wags his tail.

Zack adds a sack of Iams and a plastic bowl to the luggage. "Good boy. And this time there's nothing she can do to stop me. Come on."

Beamer hops into the passenger seat and takes inventory of Zack's luggage while Zack checks his air and oil. At first he doesn't really feel like he's running away. Not even when he stands at the pump in his favorite gas station, filling the tank.

But when he leaves the suburbs and joins I-95 North, it

all comes back. He's going to get it right this time. He's going to go where he has always belonged.

As the car accelerates and Beamer's ears begin to flap rhythmically, Zack feels a lightness and freedom he has never known before. As if some lifelong burden has finally been lifted. And he remembers his father reading *Peter Pan* to him and telling him that beautiful thoughts would give him the power to fly.

FOURTEEN

By Jacksonville he is flying low. For one thing, the sun is going down and he's still in Florida. That can't be right. After Florida he must pass through two more states. At this rate he won't get to Blue Heron Way until tomorrow. He can't spend the night at a motel because of Beamer. And he isn't going to sleep in any truck stop. Not with the movie *Hitchhike Hell* fresh in his mind.

Then there's also the issue of whether the whole idea, if you can call it that, is completely crazy. In effect, he has left his home to go to the house of a total stranger. A guy who could be a drunk or a druggie or worse; a guy who couldn't care less about his long lost son. Josh had a point this morning. Zack has been eighteen for a whole year, and not a word from this guy. Maybe he was glad to have the family off his hands. Maybe that was why, after he ran away with Zack, he brought him back. Maybe he's going to take one look at Zack and shut the door in his face. And then where will Zack be? He'll have to trudge home to Them, now a bigger traitor than before. He'll end up with nobody.

Oh, damn. Where is all that optimism he felt this

morning? Why can't he hold on to a point of view for more than ten seconds? Why is Nancy out of town?

Zack is crossing some kind of long bridge now, over a huge, vast river. The bridge goes on and on; will it never end? Zack feels a little giddy. The hood flashes in the sun, and the steering wheel seems to resist him, to pull itself out of his grip or . . . Beamer jumps up and looks at Zack anxiously. Zack hears his own heavy breathing; he's hyperventilating or something. A sea gull wheels over the car and disturbs him, startles him badly. He veers a little, hears a chorus of honks. This is a four-lane bridge. No one makes allowances for a guy having panic attacks.

Okay. Get off the bridge and pull over. But it's an endless bridge on an endless river. The sun is in his eyes, which isn't fair because he's supposed to be going north, not west. Nothing is ever, ever fair . . . Beamer barks. Adrenaline. *This is bad, Zachary. This is serious. Dangerous. You're going nuts in high-speed traffic on a four-lane bridge at rush hour. Hey, Zack! Maybe you're going to die! This could be your last mistake. What a concept.*

Beamer growls. He sees the enemy inside his friend's body. He knows he's in danger too. Zack looks at him. He can't let anything happen to Sunbeam. He has to stop, and stop right now. Now.

Zack puts on his flashers and slows, pulling over to the shoulder. Cars around him honk. "Do you mind?" he shouts at them. "I'm going crazy! Is that a good enough reason?" He slumps over the wheel, not crying or even thinking. Resting.

Beamer thinks he's sick. He applies standard dog first aid, licking any part of Zack he can get at, nuzzling the all-important face area. Zack feels sorry for him. Poor dog, stuck out here in the middle of nowhere with a loon. He puts an arm around Beamer's shoulder. Beamer settles his forepaws on Zack's knees and lowers his head for a nap.

For a long time they stay that way. Zack doesn't sleep; he watches the reddish light inside his eyelids. Every few seconds he strokes fur. Like a touchstone. A rosary. After a while his breathing is deep and regular, and the tension lifts from his body. He raises his head to see a lovely intracoastal sunset, violet over hot pink, the water below a steely, eerie blue.

"Okay," he says, which means, I'm still here. I haven't died or gone crazy. Zack does some of Nancy's breathing exercises. He feels almost calm.

Now it's just a question of whether to go on or go back. That's it. He's free to choose. If he goes on, it will be scary and uncertain. If he goes back, it will be scary and uncertain. The future, he suddenly realizes, is always like that. There's no way to play safe. There's no way to play safe.

Overhead a flock of pelicans pass in formation on their way home for the night. Zack watches their slow flight with reverence. Then he fires the engine and slowly merges into traffic on the bridge, saluted again by a chorus of honks. "Live and let live," he yells, turning on his lights and continuing north.

•

They stop for a fill-up in Savannah. At the Rougey Bros. Chevron station Zack asks how far it is to Hilton Head.

"Hitton Head? Sheeyut!" says one Rougey brother, then he turns to the other brother, and says in Georgia code, "Boah gone Hitton Head!"

The other brother wipes his nose with the back of his hand. "Huh," he says to Zack. "One owah, see? You pick you up Fowty-six in Hahdaville, then you pick you up Two-sevent'ate up by Bluffton."

Zack blinks, translating what he can. "Hilton Head is only an hour away?" he ventures.

"Yassuh!" He turns to his brother, who is ringing up Zack's gas and Snickers bar. "Hitton Head!" he chortles, as if this were a good joke.

"Yuh," agrees the other Rougey brother. "Wull," he says to Zack, tearing off his receipt. "Enjoy it, boah!"

Zack leaves in a chorus of howls, knowing he has been to an alien planet where the inhabitants have kindly spared his life.

•

Picking up "Fowty-six" in Hardeeville is easier said than done. It's a spaghetti junction, obviously the cross-roads of the South with exits in every direction. Zack exits wrong several times, gets to know the access roads of Hardeeville well, passes the same Black Cat fireworks outlet more times than he wants to. But finally he hits 46 East and heads for the coast, for his father's island.

The road is strange here, a little path through a dense forest. Just two lanes; no shoulders, no emergency call boxes. Zack finds this very unnerving. Also there are no truck stops, normal restaurants, or gas stations. Strange, ancient, gnarly trees, silhouetted against the twilight sky, form an arch across the road. Except for the occasional sign that says 46, Zack would think he had taken a wrong turn and was headed for some low-country marsh, where his car would sink into quicksand. Moss hangs from the tree branches like black lace. *The South!* Zack thinks. *This is really the South!* Every few miles a structure appears at the edge of the woods: a shack with a car sitting on blocks in front of it or a pile of rubble with a sign that says Bar-B-Q One Dollar. But mostly it's thick, dark woods, the kind of woods Dorothy and her friends were in when the flying monkeys attacked them. "I've got a feeling we're not in Kansas anymore," Zack jokes to Beamer. But Beamer is too nervous for humor. There is the sound of jabber in the woods, something between dog-baying and frog-croaking, and it makes him uneasy.

"Music," Zack suggests, turning on the radio.

John Lennon is singing "Mother."

"Or maybe not," Zack says, switching it off. The dog-frogs take over, piping in a contrapuntal rhythm something like Bach. The woods thicken, blocking out the sky completely. They seem to be all alone on this road. No car has come along in some time. A new memory tugs at Zack. About the darkness and summer nights.

•

It's dark on the back porch, comfortingly dark. Zack sits in his father's lap, half-asleep. He smells roses from Mom's trellis and beer from the open can beside them. Mom is working late, so Zack gets to stay up. The rules go kind of slack when Mom isn't around. Zack snuggles against his father's cardigan, and automatically a large hand reaches up to stroke his hair. Zack feels secure, warm, loved. He is all set for a little catnap when he sees a miracle, a tiny flash of light over the yard.

"Daddy!" Zack's body snaps to attention. "Did you see that?"

Daddy has been daydreaming as usual. "Huh?"

"Over there!" Zack points frantically into the darkness. "I saw Tinkerbell!"

"Really?" Dad squints in that direction. "Are you sure?"

There is another flash, way out at the edge of the yard. "There!" Zack shrieks with so much enthusiasm, Daddy has to cover his ears.

"I saw it," Dad says. "That's a lightning bug."

Zack is riveted to the darkness now, breathing hard. "Why?"

"Why do they call it that? Because it flashes like lightning, I guess. Hop down and you can catch one. They fly very slowly. Catch one in your hands like this." Daddy demonstrates the technique.

Zack hesitates. "Do they bite?"

"Heck no! They're friendly bugs. I wouldn't steer you wrong. Go see if you can catch one."

This is a radical idea to Zack, who has been told all his life to stay away from bugs. Sometimes Daddy has theories that don't work in reality. "You catch one first and show me," Zack coyly suggests.

Dad sighs, rises reluctantly, but then he gets into the spirit of things and starts creeping around in the dark like a stalking animal. He spots one of the bugs and puts his finger to his lips, telling Zack not to tip it off. Zack giggles. Then Daddy follows the bug around awhile, pretending to duck and hide when he thinks the bug is looking at him. Finally he swipes the air with his hands and hollers, "Gotcha!"

Zack is shrill with excitement. "Did you get him? Did you get him?"

Daddy peeks into his hands, very secretive. "Come and look for yourself." He makes a tiny opening for Zack to look through. The darkness in his hands flashes.

"Wow!" Zack says.

Daddy pulls his hands away as if guarding a treasure. "I'll let you in on a secret. These little babies grant wishes."

"Like a leprechaun?" Daddy has recently told him about the stupendous luck that comes with catching a leprechaun.

"Pretty much," Dad agrees. "What you do is, you think of something you really want. Then you whisper it to the bug and you let him go. And he flies up to heaven and whispers your wish directly to God!"

"Wow!"

"But there're two rules. Only one wish per night and you can't tell your wish to anyone."

"Are you going to wish?"

"Certainly I am. I'm not going to waste a good lightning bug." Dad puts his hands to his mouth and whispers something. Then he opens his hands, and Zack watches the little bug spread its wings and take off.

"Wow!" Zack says. "But look! He's not going toward heaven. He's going into the Sweeneys' hedge!"

"They fly around a little before they go to heaven," Dad explains. "You gonna catch one now?"

"Yes!" Zack plunges into the yard which is now thick with flashes, and turns and gazes about until he is almost dizzy. It is so magical, this hot, rose-scented night with sparkles everywhere, like little stars come to life. He can hardly believe he can really catch one. He makes a few wild passes, then tries really hard and captures one. He feels its delicate presence in his hand, and it flashes, lighting the edges of his fingers bright red. "Oh!" he cries.

"Make your wish," Dad prompts.

There is only one thing in the world Zack wants. He holds his hands over his mouth and whispers, "Golden retriever." Then he opens his hands and waits. The bug is just messing around, flipping its wings open and shut. "He won't fly!" Zack moans.

"Be patient. He's just making sure he remembers what you said. There he goes!"

Sure enough, the little bug fans its wings and ascends, flying almost straight up. "He's going right to heaven with that one!" Zack crows.

"You bet. Must have been a good one!"

Zack remembers clearly how Dad smiles when he says this and how he sees Zack looking at something behind him and how that smile just falls off his face. Daddy knows who it is. He turns and there is Mom, looking worn and tired after a long day of work and parent-teacher conferences. And instantly Dad and Zack feel guilty because they were having fun and Mom . . . hardly ever has fun.

"Hi." Dad sounds like a little boy talking to his mom.

"Hi," she says, not friendly. "What's Zachary doing up this late?"

Zack wants to help Dad out, wants to make her understand. "We were catching lightning bugs and sending them to heaven."

She glances at Dad and then back to Zack. "What?"

"Daddy showed me. You tell them your wish and they fly to heaven and tell God."

Mom and Dad look at each other.

"What if he repeated something like that in church?" Mom says in a tight voice.

They look at each other some more.

"The foundations of Christianity would crumble?" Dad suggests.

"Very funny," she says. "Very funny. Is it too much to ask that if I go away one night you put him to bed on time?"

"Looks that way," Dad says.

"I suppose you've been drinking too."

"Oh, yeah. Knocked off a case of Scotch. Right before the prostitutes came. Well, no. Zack had *some* of the Scotch. But don't worry. I told him to stay away from the prostitutes . . ." That's as far as he gets because she has turned away. She takes Zack's hand and hauls him toward the house.

Dad sits back down on the porch and picks up his beer. "Shit," he says.

Mom drags Zack through the living room and down the hall; he's afraid she's going to spank him because she is really mad. "I didn't do anything, did I?" he pleads. She doesn't spank often, but when it happens, you remember it.

She hauls him into the bathroom. "Wash your hands," she says, pulling his step-up to the sink. "I can smell those filthy bugs on you."

Zack turns on the tap and starts washing his hands, but she isn't satisfied. She grabs his hands and scrubs them herself. Hard. It hurts a little. Zack is getting angry.

"They aren't filthy bugs! They fly up to heaven and talk to God!"

"They don't do any such thing," she says. "You say

your *prayers* to God and He hears you. You don't need any bugs doing it for you. They're just bugs. Daddy made the whole thing up. You can't believe anything he says."

"Oh," says Zack. He wants to argue but he can't. Sometimes Daddy does say things that turn out not to be true. It's very confusing. "Why does he do that?"

"I don't know." She carries Zack across the hall; strips him and puts on his pajamas with perfect efficiency; kisses Josh, kisses Zack, flips off the light and is gone.

Zachary can't sleep. What good is a father if you can't believe anything he says? Fathers are supposed to explain everything. Anyway, maybe Mom doesn't know everything either. Maybe Dad knows something about bugs that she doesn't know. She's not so hot. Because he's been praying for a golden retriever for over a year and so far it's been zip. Sometimes he has the disquieting feeling that neither one of them has a good grip on things. And where does that leave him? Nowhere.

•

Zack surfaces just in time to notice he's in Bluffton and needs to change roads again. Signs are now mentioning Hilton Head. It's thirteen miles away. He's thirteen miles away from his father.

That memory explains a lot. The confusion Zack has always felt about everything. It comes from them. They were opposites and they tried to teach him two opposite ways to look at the world. The part of himself he has always felt guilty about, that's his father-part, buried and struggling to surface. That's why he's here now. He has got to see that father-part or he'll never be whole.

The woods suddenly give way to open grasslands. He knows he's approaching the shore. He wishes one of those memories had yielded up the tiger image, but it's still a mystery. Maybe he will ask his father. Maybe it will mean something to him. If his father lets him in.

A causeway. This is it. He's leaving the mainland, crossing the bridge to his father's island. No turning back. The sign says Welcome to Hilton Head. Zack stops at a gas station for directions. The whole island, he is told, is divided into "plantations." They seem to be like little fiefdoms. The gas station attendant, who speaks a whole new kind of English, gives Zack an island map and explains: Hilton Head is shaped like a boot. Blue Heron Way is part of Sea Pines Plantation, down in the toe of the boot. Zack will have to navigate two traffic circles and pay a three-dollar entrance fee to get to his dad.

As he drives through Hilton Head, Zack sees what the Rougey brothers were laughing at. Hilton Head is some kind of rich people's resort, with just little pieces of normal town here and there. The plantations dominate, one after the other, huge hotel-eating-shopping complexes, all with their own marina and beach. The whole place has been zoned like crazy to imply luxury and aesthetics, which Zack is not crazy about because the streetlights are low and indirect. It's unnerving for someone trying to find his way. There are no billboards, no big neon signs. Even the McDonald's has tiny arches in its front yard instead of the big ones. The people on this island have enough money to tell McDonald's what to do!

At the entrance to Sea Pines a guard protects the road from vagrants and poor people. Zack explains himself, pays three dollars, and gets a one-day pass for his windshield. As he drives on, the guard salutes him.

Now he is in a residential area, and even at night Zack can see this is the loveliest neighborhood in the world. Woods and streams, a golf course here and there, tasteful signs pointing to the beach. All the houses are masterpieces of architecture with redwood siding and widow's walks and porthole windows. Most of the mailboxes are redwood! How did his father, the bum, end up here?

All the streets have pretty names. Camellia Place, Osprey Drive. Named by developers instead of real people. Zack realizes the next cross street is Blue Heron Way. He's here. His heart begins doing scary things. Zack reminds himself he's too young to be at risk for a heart attack. He tries to practice his breathing exercises, but he chokes and gives it up.

He turns into his father's street. The house is three doors down, a Victorian loaded with gingerbread. On the roof, a weather vane with a little whimsical whale. All around the front, some kind of tall hedge with just a little opening to walk through. Zack parks in the street and just sits there awhile. The lights are on. Somebody's home. Zack looks at Beamer. "Should we do it?" he asks, as if hoping the dog will talk him out of it. But Beamer is road-weary and looks hopeful.

176

Zack gets out of the car. The neighborhood is quiet except for the rhythmic barking of those Carolina dog-frogs. The air is sultry and damp, heavy with the scent of the hedges. Zack walks up a gravel path, looking at his feet. His duffel and his dog bump comfortingly against his legs. He suddenly wonders how he looks as a kid. Is he the kind of kid you'd want to claim? What do fathers want their sons to look like? In the next minute he'll know. He'll see some kind of expression on this man's face, and he'll know if he's okay.

Zack stands on the porch listening to his father's television set. A burst of sit-com laughter. Zack rings the bell. "If you've ever loved me," he whispers to Beamer, "don't piss on anything when he comes to the door."

A porch light hits Zack and blinds him. The front door opens and there's the man of Zack's dreams, the star of his flashbacks. Anthony Lloyd: tall, blond, affable, vague. Khaki shorts, white T-shirt. In good shape for his age. Barefoot, needing a haircut, yawning, looking puzzled at finding a strange boy on his porch with a dog and a duffel bag.

Then the vague look fades and something keen and intelligent takes its place; his eyes suddenly resemble Zachary's. Zack has never seen such an intense look, except maybe Clara's when she was making love to him. The man is staring, gazing, spellbound. "Zachary?" he whispers.

Zachary feels like crying. "Yeah," he tries to say, but the word splinters on his outrushing breath.

And the big man throws the screen door out of the way and pulls Zack into his arms, crushing and hugging. And into Zack's shoulder he moans the last piece of the puzzle. "Oh, Tiger, is that really you?"

FIFTEEN

Dragged inside by his bear-hugging father, Zack stumbles, half blinded by track lighting and tears. The living room is predictable—taupes, beiges, modern sculpture. But there are two big surprises: first, a larger-than-life portrait of Zack over the couch, and second, a leggy blond lady *on* the couch. Zack doesn't know which one to stare at first.

His father has still not let go, is holding Zack by the shoulders now. "This is my son!" he cries to the lady.

The blond lady gracefully sits up, aims the remote control to turn off the TV, smiles at Zack, looks up at his portrait and back down. "I believe you're right," she says with an English accent. "It is."

"Zack, this is Eleanor Montgomery," his father says. "She's my . . . friend."

"Hello, Zack," says Eleanor Montgomery. Her smile is at once amused, cynical, predatory, and warm. She would be a wonderful portrait subject, Zack thinks.

Meanwhile Beamer has gone crazy in the new environment and is barking his head off. Zachary pulls gently out of his father's grasp and kneels, hugging the dog and trying to quiet him. Really, it is just an excuse. This is all too much, too confusing. He needs a minute to think.

"What are you doing here?" his father says. "Does your mother know you're here?"

Afraid to look around, Zack shakes his head no.

"What's wrong?" his father asks, his voice raised slightly with anxiety. "What's going on?"

Zack freezes up. This guy is kind of pushy for a total stranger. You can't just answer a question like that in a couple of words. "I don't know," he says. The dog has walked away, toward Eleanor, but Zack is still kneeling with his back to his father, like a prisoner waiting for the lash.

Eleanor takes charge. "You know what? I think the two of you need a moment alone. What if I take Sunbeam out to the porch and get him settled?"

Zack looks at her, sees from the way she is fondling Sunbeam's ears that she is an animal person. You can always tell. "How do you know my dog's name?" he asks softly.

She laughs, rises, slips two fingers under Beamer's collar. "We know lots of things about you." She laughs again. "You'd be surprised. Come on, old man." She leads Beamer toward a sliding glass door.

"Where's Dandelion?" Zack's father asks her.

"She's out for the evening, don't worry," Eleanor says. "She won't be back till much later." She opens the glass door with her foot and guides Beamer through.

Zack stands up and looks at his father. It is hard not to stare.

"This is weird," his father says.

"Yeah," Zack whispers. It is. His father's eyes are a different color, gray; but otherwise, they are Zack's eyes. It is like looking in a mirror—a feeling he never has with Mom and Josh, who have sweet, round, baby eyes. These eyes are restless, wolfish. It is both thrilling and disturbing to see a part of oneself on a stranger's body. The hands and fingernails are the same too. And the feet.

"Tell me what you're doing here," his father urges gently. "I didn't think you even . . ."

"Did you paint that?" Zack asks, turning to his portrait. He isn't ready for questions yet.

"Yes."

Zack approaches and studies it. From the angle and expression he sees it's his senior picture, romanticized with halos of light. "You must have just painted this."

"Yeah. She sends me pictures of you every once in a while. I've done several paintings of you over the years. You make a good subject."

"Thank you," Zack says, feeling foolish. This is a dumb conversation to be having at a moment like this. Then he sees something else. "You paint in oils?"

"Yeah," his father says, almost apologetically. "I like them better. The blending."

Zack touches his heart. "*I* paint in oils too. Isn't that weird?"

"Definitely weird. I didn't think anybody but me painted in oils nowadays."

Zack is still looking at the painting. "I remembered you were an artist. I've been remembering all kinds of things. That's why . . . I'm here. Did you know I was an artist?" He turns to his father. It is getting easier to look into those eyes now.

"Of course. I know all about you. Mary . . . we write to each other. I know you just won a prize."

"Yeah. First prize. I was the best in my school."

His father smiles. "I'm proud of you."

The words go through Zack's body like a splash of sunlight. But is it just a stock phrase? "I'm . . . angry . . ." he says, twisting his hands, ". . . because she didn't even tell me you were a painter. It would have been— If I'd known . . ."

"Sit down and tell me what's going on," his father says. "I'm real confused here. I thought you didn't know anything about me."

"I didn't. I . . . Then last year I started having dreams. They were about you. And I began therapy and I started remembering more and more. And I made her tell me the truth . . . She wanted us to think you were *dead*!"

Mr. Lloyd lowers his eyes. "I know."

"Why would you go along with that?"

"It's a long story. I'll try to explain it to you."

"I made her tell me the truth, and I found your address and then I had to come because . . ."

"Of course you did. Look, we're going to sort all of this out, but right now let's call Mary and tell her where you are so she won't freak out. I don't need the FBI up here on my ass."

"No! I mean, don't call her. I don't want to talk to her. I can't . . ." He suddenly feels like he's going to cry and he blushes with shame. He must look like a total idiot to this man.

"Mary needs to know where you are, okay? You don't have to come to the phone. I'll handle it." That seems to be the end of the discussion because he picks up the telephone and balances it in his lap, punching up the number from memory. How often does he call? Zack realizes the phone must have rung sometimes when he was right there in the house, and if he had only picked it up, it would have been his father.

"Mary?" Dad clears his throat. "Yes, it's me. Zack's up here . . . Okay, calm down. He's fine. . . . What? . . . No, we were out for a while. I didn't look at my messages. . . . I'm sure you were. . . . I know, but he's eighteen. It isn't that far a drive. . . . I don't know, maybe you can tell me. . . . He's fine, I said, just fine. Mary, believe me, I can tell when a person is all right. He's not sobbing or wielding a knife or *anything*. . . . Yep, the dog's here too. . . . Well, I don't know. We haven't discussed his long-range plans. . . . No. He doesn't want to. He told me already he doesn't want to. . . . I don't know why. Look, he's confused. He's been through a lot, right? Can't

183

you be just a little . . ." He sighs and puts his hand over the mouthpiece. "She really wants to talk to you."

Zack squirms.

"He doesn't want to. Not right now, anyway. Look, I think he probably just wants to spend a little time here and . . . sort things out. This is weird for him. It's weird for all of us. . . . Well, I wouldn't know about that, would I? I just wanted to tell you he's all right. . . . What?" He sighs again and covers the mouthpiece. "She wants you to know your girlfriend called."

Zack frowns. "I don't have a girlfriend."

"I told him. Any other messages? . . . Yes, Mary, I realize that. I'm the one that *pays* for his therapy. But really, dear, I can tell the difference between troubled and psychotic. . . . I will. I'll call you tomorrow. Okay? . . . How's Josh? . . . Well, sure he is but. . . . Okay, just a sec." He heaves a deep sigh as he covers the mouthpiece. "You want to talk to Josh?"

Zack shakes his head.

"Three strikes you're out, Mary. . . . Well, that's too bad! I'd really like to say that you brought this on your-self, but I'm too cool to do that. Just relax. . . . Well, do the best you can. I'll call you. Bye." He hangs up quickly. "Brrr," he comments to Zack.

Zack hugs himself. "Is she mad?"

"No, she's just worried about you."

"What? She thinks I've gone crazy or something?"

"Well, she's always had the feeling that if you really

remembered me, it would plunge you into madness. Not a compliment to me, I must say."

"I'm not crazy," Zack says. "I mean, if I'm acting weird, it's because . . . this is weird."

"I know. Don't worry."

"Can I really stay here awhile? Maybe a few days? I mean, I'd like to get to know you a little."

"Well, no shit!"

Zack laughs. "What about your . . . friend? Will she mind?"

"Eleanor? Of course not. Dandelion might be a problem . . ."

"Who's that, her daughter?"

"Her cat."

"Oh."

With timing that suggests eavesdropping Eleanor reappears from the sun porch, tying her hair back with a scarf. She has an angular beauty that would best be captured in pen and ink, and a lazy, catlike grace. Her white tennis shorts show off long, tanned legs. Zack admires his father's taste. "Sunbeam is taking a nap," she announces. "He's all tuckered out from his journey. Are we getting nicely acquainted?"

"Starting to," Dad says. There is an eagerness in his voice when he speaks to her. Wherever she goes in the room, his body seems to lean in that direction. Zack can see his father is in love.

Eleanor perches on a chair and looks at him through narrowed eyes. "How is Mary?"

Dad smiles a little. "Beside herself."

"Good heavens, not two of her!" Eleanor exclaims. She looks at Zack. "I'll bet you're hungry."

He is. "Well . . ."

"What kind of sandwich do you like? Ham? Tuna?"

"Tuna. If it isn't too much trouble."

"Oh, it's quite a hassle opening the can. Coffee? Milk? Coke?"

"Just water."

"Come on. How about—" She looks at him slyly. "—chocolate milk with ice cubes."

Zack shivers. "I'd love that."

She smiles her cryptic smile. "Thought you would." She bobs up and exits with such grace it forces both men to stare after her.

Zack's father sighs, lovesick. Then he turns to Zack. "Do you remember chocolate milk with ice cubes?"

Zack shakes his head.

Dad looks disappointed. "You loved it when you were little. You used to order it in restaurants."

"It sounds great. But how does *she* know?"

Mr. Lloyd blushes. "I guess I talk about that stuff a lot."

There is a brief silence.

"Why did you let me think you were dead?" Zack says quietly.

His father looks up. Scared. Guilty. "I didn't want to. I mean, how much do you remember? Do you remember that we—that day I took you away?"

"Yes."

"Well. Mary had me arrested. She had me put in fucking *jail*. Excuse me. I didn't mean to use that word."

"It's okay."

"She . . . I never dreamed she'd be so vindictive. I mean, what I did was wrong and all that, but . . . anyway, she pressed criminal charges. The laws have changed a little, but in those days I could have been charged with a felony. You know? Prison. Hard time. I was scared out of my mind. So while I was in jail thinking that over, she came to me with a divorce thing and also some paper where she wanted me to agree that I was an unfit father and to let her have sole custody. So she got a judgment against me and I couldn't contact you as long as you were a minor. You or Josh. And that was that. She sends me pictures and clippings and copies of your report cards. And I pay child support and buy a few extras for you, like Joshua's music lessons and your car—"

"You paid for my car?"

"Yeah. Anyway, that's all I'm allowed to do."

"But I turned eighteen last winter."

"I know. The moment I'd been waiting for. I had speeches planned, things I wanted to say. I called Mary, and first she gave me some story like I should wait two more years until you're *both* over eighteen, and I told her I'd get a lawyer and see about that. But then she got something better. She told me about your nightmares and your emotional problems and how you were in therapy because the 'kidnapping' was so traumatic to you.

She gave me all her usual arguments about how you had accepted the idea I was dead, and you were fragile now, and if I showed up, it might do you some kind of harm."

Zack takes a deep breath. "I think I'm having problems because she's been lying to me all these years."

"Well, that's what I'd like to think too. But . . . I don't know. It's hard to stand up to Mary. She always seems so good and virtuous and she makes me feel like some kind of—pardon me—shit. I mean, she was the one who raised you, and in a lot of ways I *was* an unfit father. I felt guilty about what I'd done, trying to take you away. I don't know. I was scared to do anything." He looks down at his hands. "That sounds kind of weak, doesn't it?"

There is another short silence.

Zack's hand strays toward his father, touching him lightly on the arm. "She does that to me too."

Again showing excellent timing, Eleanor reappears with a marmalade cat around her shoulders. "Look who popped in the back window when I opened the tuna can." She gives the cat to Zack's father, goes back to the kitchen, and returns with Zack's sandwich and his frosted chocolate milk.

"I made you a sandwich, too, glutton," she says to Zachary's father. "You want the usual to drink?"

"Yes, please." He puts the cat down, and it runs to the sliding glass door, where it grunts and paws the carpet. "Calm down," he says. "You'll get to meet the doggie soon enough." He turns back to Zack. "It's funny you named your dog Sunbeam."

Zack is savoring his drink. He knows from the way he loves it it is something from long ago. "Why?"

"'Cause I used to say to you, when you were sulking, 'Where's my Sunbeam?' and I would tease you like that until you smiled. Do you think you remembered that, or is it just a coincidence?"

"I don't know," Zack says with his mouth full. Eleanor makes a mean tuna sandwich. Not too much mayonnaise and a little garlic powder.

She brings in another sandwich, a can of beer, and a glass of something magenta. Zack expects the beer to go to his dad, but Eleanor keeps that for herself.

"What is that?" Zack points to his father's colorful drink. "A mai-tai?"

The adults laugh. "Kool-Aid," Dad says. "I'm a recovering alcoholic."

"Your father has been sober for six years," Eleanor says. "You should be proud of him." She sips her beer and lights a cigarette.

"I am," Zack says.

"Eleanor did it," Dad says. "I never considered going for treatment until I met her. She is definitely not an enabler."

Eleanor grins. "I'm a hand-smacker."

Zack looks at his father. "Are you going to help her quit smoking?"

Zack's father laughs. "I'm afraid I am an enabler."

Eleanor takes a puff, tossing back her fine hair. "Lucky for me," she says, winking at Zack.

They talk about normal things for a while—school, art, Joshua, Zack's car. He learns Eleanor is a stockbroker, and it is implied she is Dad's unofficial art dealer and business manager as well. He is successful on a small scale, supplies the gift shops around Hilton Head with what he calls "too-rist" paintings, but has a few good things placed in galleries and homes. He loves Hilton Head and seems contented. There is obvious chemistry between him and Eleanor although they show it by taunting and teasing each other. He says her cat is a pain in the ass. She says he's too stupid to play golf. They never touch each other, but the way they make eye contact speaks volumes. They've been together six years but don't plan to marry. "We already have a toaster-oven," Zack's father explains.

When the food is finished, Eleanor cleans up and then excuses herself to prepare the guest room. Zack appreciates her discretion. She makes him feel welcome, but she thoughtfully makes herself as scarce as possible so Zack and his father can talk.

"Want to meet my dog?" Zack asks his dad.

Dad glances down the hall, sees that Dandelion has followed her mother into the guest room. "Okay."

Zack opens the glass door. Beamer gallops out, sniffs the air and aims himself toward the guest room. "Noooooo!" Zack says, grabbing his collar and dragging him back. "You can meet the kitty later. This is my dad."

Forced to look at Mr. Lloyd, Beamer finally takes an interest. He cocks his head and stares. Perhaps he sees a facial resemblance to Zack or smells the same DNA or something. He respectfully licks Mr. Lloyd's hand.

Zack's father pats Beamer nicely, but he's not an animal person. You can tell. His first flaw. But Zack knows true animal people are quite rare, so it's okay. "He's a beautiful dog," Dad says as if apologizing for his deficiency.

"He's a year and a half old," Zack says proudly.

"I know. I gave him to you for your seventeenth birthday."

Zack puts his arms around Beamer and buries his face in fur. For a moment he is overwhelmed. He realizes now he and his dad are not in the same situation at all. He is just beginning to remember his father. His father never forgot him for a second.

•

They settle him in a guest room done in nautical-trite —blue bedspread, braided rug, brass accents. On the walls are Dad's "too-rist" watercolors of striped lighthouses and terns. Beamer sleeps with Zack so Dandelion can have her sun porch. Dad says he's getting up early in the morning to sketch. Would Zack like to come along? Zack would. Dad and Eleanor say good night to him from the doorway, like Ozzie and Harriet, and then he is suddenly alone in a dark room in a strange house with no Joshua asking stupid questions and no Mom prowling the halls and making him nervous. Zack hates to admit it, but he misses home a little. These people use a different laundry detergent. The sheets don't smell like home. The fixtures in the yellow bathroom where he brushed his teeth were confusing. Even the ship's clock on the bookshelf seems to be ticking funny. Zack calls Beamer and gathers him in his arms for security.

Dad and Eleanor sleep next door. He can faintly hear their voices through the wall, but Zack is too honorable to get up and eavesdrop. They are probably talking about him, and he doesn't want to hear. Even if they are happy about it, this is a surprise and they have to react. The main thing is, he can tell they aren't arguing. Then he hears Eleanor laugh and there is something like scuffling.

"Uh-oh," he says to Beamer.

More giggling, both male and female. Without even meaning to, Zack pictures it. His father's big body sprawled out on the bed; Eleanor, lean and athletic, wearing trim white cotton underwear. His father playfully pulling the underwear down. A wrestling match. Bodies rolling around . . . Zack feels a sharp tug in the crotch. He squirms. This is indecent!

He pushes Beamer aside and reaches over to turn on his bedside radio. The first thing he gets is "Top 40," which is naturally a song about how much some man wants some woman, but he fiddles with the dial and finds Mozart. He cranks it up loud enough to drown out any noises that might come through the wall. Then he lies down carefully on his back and thinks about the multiplication tables until the throbbing in his groin recedes to the dull ache of frustration. And then he thinks of Clara. Tears spill from the corners of his closed eyes.

SIXTEEN

A shower is running somewhere.

Zack opens his eyes in the strange room. Last night seems like years ago. He sits up, alerting Beamer, who is already awake and at the window gazing at the strange lawn. Zack joins him, yawning. The view is startling. That tall thick hedge he saw last night—it must be six feet high and circles the entire property—is loaded with the lurid magenta blooms of azaleas. The visual impact is almost frightening. Zack determines from the noisy bird songs and the dew on the grass that it is just after sunrise. He slept fitfully last night, but with no nightmares. There hasn't been a single nightmare since he remembered his father.

The shower down the hall stops. Zack hugs himself. He is miles from home. These people are really strangers to him. Another shower starts up.

Zack picks up the telephone. He thinks he is calling home, but he dials Clara's number instead. As it rings he prepares himself to slam it down at the first sound of her voice.

"Hello?" she says.

He freezes, holding his breath. Her East Coast accent

undoes him; brings back memories of her lilac scent, her body heat, her smile.

"Hello?" she says angrily. She thinks it's a pervert.

"Hi."

"Zachary?"

"Hi."

"Where *are* you? Your mother said you ran away!"

"I'm with my dad." Goose bumps from the phrase.

"Your dad? Where's that? How did you find him?"

"South Carolina. I just did."

Long silence. Static.

"Well . . ." she says. "What's going on? Do you like him?"

"I don't know what's going on. Yeah, I do."

Her voice gets small. "When are you coming back?"

"I don't know."

Loud static. Somebody's using a hair dryer.

"*Are* you coming back?"

"I don't know."

It sounds like she's breathing hard. "Well . . . why are you calling?"

"You called *me*. I'm returning your call."

"Oh."

"What did you want?"

"Oh. I guess I wanted to say I was sorry. About graduation day, when you told me all this stuff. I was too wrapped up in myself and I wasn't there for you."

"Oh."

"So I'm sorry, okay?"

"Okay."

She exhales. "Well, have fun up there."

He takes a deep breath. "I miss you."

Her voice breaks. "Me too."

Zack wonders if he's holding up breakfast or anything. "I might call you again."

"Okay."

"Okay, well, I'd better go."

"Okay."

"Okay. Good-bye."

"Good-bye."

"Good-bye."

"I love you!" she blurts, and hangs up.

Zack holds the receiver, watching it tremble.

•

He takes a long, hot shower, shaves twice, and takes great pains with the part in his hair. He puts on blue jeans, a white T-shirt, Keds, careful to project no particular image. Then he feeds Beamer in his room to stall for time. Finally he feels ready to face a strange household.

At first the house is so quiet, he thinks everyone's gone. As he goes down the hall, he can't help glancing into rooms. The bedroom where they did the deed last night. Sleigh bed. Antique quilts. Primitive art. "The Tiger Orchard" would hang well in this room.

The next doorway is his father's studio. Zack steps across the threshold, inhaling deeply. Linseed oil, turpentine, cedar. Sink, paper towels. Long worktable. Stack of newspapers. Mr. Coffee. A boom box. Canvases stacked everywhere. A Far Side calendar. Pencil sketches framed and hanging on the wall. Zachary and Joshua, maybe six and eight years old, done from photographs. He steps farther into the room to see what's hanging on the blind wall. A framed watercolor of Eleanor. Nude, but tasteful. Wow.

"You up, Tiger?" Dad calls from somewhere.

Zack jumps guiltily away from the painting and scuttles back into the hall. "Yeah!" He follows the direction of the voice through the living room and a big, high-tech kitchen, into a little breakfast room with sliding glass doors that face onto another section of the azalea hedge. Also a white statue of Saint Francis of Assisi.

Dad is seated at an oak table, reading a newspaper. He, too, is wearing blue jeans and a white T-shirt. Still barefoot. Does this guy ever wear shoes? He looks up at Zack and grins, as naturally as if they had been having breakfast together for the past eighteen years. "Hi!"

"Hi!" Zack tries to match his dad's brightness. He pulls out a chair, inventories the table, gets his bearings. Dad's a slob—gouged butter, bread crumbs everywhere, knife stuck in the marmalade jar like Excalibur. Marmalade is Zack's favorite spread too. Genetics is strange.

Shyly Zack takes a piece of toast and butters it.

"Sleep well?" Dad asks, still reading.

"Sure." Zack gets up to pour himself some coffee.

"Really? Boy, I envy you. I can't sleep in a strange place. I would have been up all night."

Zack returns with his coffee. The sun's angle has shifted; light now streams across the table. This room must face east. Zack feels a sudden rush. This is nice. He's on vacation. He can do anything he wants. "Did Eleanor go to work?"

Mr. Lloyd puts down the paper and salutes. "Oh, yes! The empire would crumble if Eleanor didn't clock in on time. She's a complete workaholic. Climb the rope! Ring the bell!"

Zack giggles. "Not like you."

Dad laughs. "Not hardly. But give me credit. I'm vertical before noon! That's something. I plan to do some work today, when I'm not busy taking in the sight of my handsome, grown-up son."

Zack blushes.

"You know what's funny? You're still the same."

"How so?"

"It's weird. Physically you're a different person from this little five-year-old I knew. But yet you're the same. All your little gestures and expressions. You know? It's like I don't know you, but I do."

"You don't know me that well," Zack says. "I'm hard to know."

Dad grins. "Yeah? Want a demonstration?"

Zack laughs. "Take your best shot."

"Okay . . . how's this? You didn't sleep well at all. You just *said* you did."

Zack blushes again. "How did you know?"

"That's what you do. You're a stoic. You always say

everything is all right, to avoid trouble. It used to be my job to tell if you were being honest or not. See, if you had said *yes* when I asked you if you slept well, I would have believed you. But you said *sure*. That meant you were lying. Impressed?"

"Humbled! It took me and my therapist six months to figure that out. Why do I do it?"

His father smiles. "I said I understood how you work. I don't know why."

Zack takes a sip of his coffee. "That's more than Mom can do."

His father looks at him. "I know." Then he drops his eyes suddenly. "I want to explain to you . . . See, you were always like . . . my kid, and Josh was . . . like hers. That sounds wrong, but it really wasn't such a bad arrangement. How much of this do you remember?"

"I know you and I were close," Zack says softly.

"We were. I think it's because right after you were born your Mom wanted to go right back to work. I think she needed to prove something to herself. You know, that having a kid hadn't derailed her career."

"Uh-huh." Zack wants to encourage this. Every scrap of information is like gold.

"So, there I was in the house, being your caretaker. So we must have done that bonding thing, you know?"

"You did everything? Feeding and changing and stuff?"

"Everything. I loved it. I took to it. Or rather, I took to you. From the very start we clicked. I had never thought I'd be the parental type, but I *was*. Once you arrived, I lost my head. I stared at you night and day. I was crazy about you. And it just got better and better. Because you were becoming more of a person every day and after a while we could talk . . . it was like . . . I don't know. I can't explain. Just take the best friendship you ever had in your life and multiply it by a thousand. That was how I felt about you."

Zack knows. He remembers the feeling. Being adored. "You didn't feel that way about Josh?"

"This is just between us."

"I know."

"Okay, it wasn't the same. For one thing, the year he was born, your mother was fed up with my being unemployed and she made me get a job, so she stayed home with him. I'll tell you frankly, she was getting jealous of you and me and what we had going. So I ended up in a boiler room selling magazines over the phone—I've never had a decent job in my life—and she played mommy for a while."

"I see," Zack says. Don't let him run down. Keep him talking. This is vital.

Mr. Lloyd sits back in his chair, cradling his coffee in both hands. "That was the worst year of my life, Zack. Our family income dropped dramatically, since I made half what your mother made. I missed you. I was doing a shitty job that I hated. Mary was irritable. I couldn't sell a painting to save my life. I was too tired to make new paintings. That was when I started drinking. And . . . I had an affair."

"Oh." Zack doesn't like this.

"I know. But I was messed up. I hated my whole life. She was nobody, just a body. Just an escape from reality. Plus she loved to get crocked as much as I did. It was awful. Sometimes I stayed away from home for weeks at a time."

"I don't remember much of this."

"Good. Anyway, finally Mary and I talked the whole thing out and we agreed she needed to go back to work and I needed to stay home and paint. So that helped a little, but I still couldn't make it as a painter. So I stayed sober during the day when I was responsible for you. But every night I would drink a six-pack and pass out. I was Jekyll and Hyde. Finally Mary got fed up. I was a great nanny, but that's it. I wasn't a lover to her, I couldn't hold even the dumbest job. She hated the moods I got into about my art, and she had to undress me and put me to bed every night. You can't blame her for getting sick of it. So she told me to get out." He begins stacking all the dishes in his vicinity, putting things in order.

"And that's when . . . we ran away from home?"

Dad is still now. "Zachary. I'm sorry. I'm really, really sorry."

Zack looks at him. "For what?"

"For doing that. Running away with you. I just . . . loved you, but it was wrong. All the trouble it caused you, the way it messed you up. . . . When I heard you were in therapy. . . . I never meant to do that to you, Tiger."

The sun is high in the sky now; the lawn sparkles.

Beamer pads into the kitchen, sniffing things, following the cat's trail. He finds a little cat-size water bowl and turns his head this way and that, trying to fit his muzzle in.

"Dad . . ." Zack says, and the word hits him hard. He pauses for a minute, shuddering from the recoil.

"What?"

Zack looks at him. "I don't think you understand. I *was* blocking a bad memory, but it wasn't running away with you. It's what happened afterward, the way she sicced the cops on you and they . . ." His voice wobbles. ". . . hit you and pushed you and took you away."

"You saw that? I thought you were in the house."

"I saw it. This is really important for you to understand. This is the whole thing. I'm not screwed up because you tried to take me away from her. I'm screwed up because she tried to take me away from *you*!"

They lock eyes. Lapping noises fill the quiet kitchen.

"I needed you!" Zack insists, suddenly aware of tears running down his face. "When you were gone . . . I was . . . lost. You know what I mean?"

Anthony Lloyd gets up, takes a stack of dishes to the sink. "Boy," he says softly. "Do I!"

•

Water sparkles in the Calibogue Sound. Sparkles that run to infinity, melt against the horizon. This is too easy, too paradisiacal. Some kind of mistake has been made. Zack was in the middle of a tense, repressed, nightmare-

202

haunted life. Now a needle has skipped somewhere in the cosmos and all the strings are cut. Total freedom. Total bliss. It just can't be. Life just isn't this simple.

They are in a place called Harbourtown, the mother of all tourist traps, Dad says, dominated by a cute little candy-striped lighthouse. Spreading out behind it, a network of docks, decks, marinas, and souvenir shops that carry Dad's paintings, galleries that carry his real paintings, ice cream kiosks, cappuccino huts, condos, golf courses, and the Crazy Crab restaurant, where Dad has promised him lunch when he's finished "performing." Performing means standing at an easel on the dock, acting like a Local Artist on the Scene, chatting with tourists, and directing them to the gift shops where his paintings can be found. One lady makes her husband take her picture with Zack's father, like he's just another tree or rock. "Don't you feel used?" Zack asks.

"Yeah!" his father says. "It's great!"

That's the kind of lunatic he is. Right now as he artfully washes a blue sky into his picture of the sound, he is bouncing from one foot to the other, singing to himself like a madman. "Lollipop, lollipop, oh lolly lolly lolly . . ."

And this kind of thing is infectious. Zack, the original Ice Man, is thawing rapidly. He feels relaxed as hell sitting on the dock with one foot propped up, sketching his sleeping dog, watching waves of wind roll through the marsh grass, gazing at the slow drift of sailboats. Why can't life be easy? Why can't it be fun? What was all that anxiety about?

"Look!" Dad cries. Every ten minutes he exclaims about something. The whole world seems to amaze him. Now it's a blackbird landing in an oyster bed, flipping shells with its beak.

And Zack smiles because it *is* awesome and wonderful. "Yeah!" he agrees.

Beamer sees the bird; jumps up and begins to bark.

"No!" Zack says. "Bad dog!"

Dad laughs. "Let him have his fun."

There it is, Zack thinks. *My father's philosophy*.

And the blackbird flips a shell high in the air, showering beads of water like tiny diamonds.

•

The Crazy Crab is cool and shadowy after the dazzle outside. Here amidst fishnets and anchors Zack is initiated into the mysteries of she-crab soup.

"So how did you end up here?" Zack asks, crumbling oyster crackers. This stuff is *good*.

His father never really eats. He plays with food, takes it apart, moves it around. Mostly he drinks iced tea. The waiter has filled his glass about sixteen times. "I didn't come here at first. I went to Atlanta."

"Georgia? Why?"

"Bright lights, big city. It was on I-seventy-five. Who knows? Anyway, once there I spent several minutes trying to be taken seriously as an artist, then I embarked on a full-time career as a self-destructive alcoholic. I worked in various bars, getting fired each time the management caught on."

"Boy."

"And getting sicker by the minute. You vomit and pass out on a regular basis, it takes a toll. I looked like the wrong end of the picture of Dorian Gray."

"So what happened?"

Dad grins. He likes this story. "Eleanor. I had landed an unusually good busboy job in a trendy little Buckhead bar—Buckhead is the suburb of Atlanta where the hotshots hang out."

Zack nods.

"Eleanor was there with some spiffy female friends. A table of gorgeous, classy women. A perfect target for Tony Lloyd, obnoxious drunk."

"God."

"Even with double vision my gaze was focused on Eleanor. She was my Beatrice, my ideal. Grace Kelly with a whip. I loved her all the way across the room. So I staggered over and tried to impress her by making inarticulate attempts at human speech."

Zack tries not to laugh but can't help it. "Are you exaggerating all this?"

"Not much. I was *lit*. I was brain-fried. She could probably tell you better than me exactly how much of a fool I was acting. In my mind I was Cary Grant. But I'm sure what was coming out was Quasimodo. Her friends were all laughing in my face, but not Eleanor. She was just watching and listening. I thought I was getting somewhere."

Zack is forgetting to eat. "Then what?"

"Then I did what I always did at the stroke of midnight. I blacked out. I remember the table hitting my jaw."

"Wow."

"Yeah, wow. So anyway, cut to the following morning. I woke up in a clean, well-lighted place. Eleanor's place."

"Yeah?"

"Yeah. She'd brought me home, cleaned me up, put me to bed. She came in the room, brought me coffee, and started lecturing. She hasn't stopped since. I love it." He pauses to rattle his ice and drain off the last of his tea.

"Why'd she do it?"

"I never knew. I just took it for a miracle. I never really understood until a couple of years ago when she brought Dandelion home. Same deal. Feral cat, wandering on the docks, ear torn in a fight, covered in mud. That cat looked like hell. You saw her last night. She's a vision now. She could probably win ribbons. Eleanor likes to recycle things. She takes garbage and reclaims it. She told me, in that first lecture, that she'd been able to discern from my bleary remarks, I was intelligent. She says I used the word 'fortuitous.' She said no man with a good vocabulary like that should be wrecking his life. Then she saw my paintings and really went to town. Started taking my stuff around to the galleries. She's pushy. I can't act like that. She got me in and pretty soon I was a modest success.

She made me get in a program, get sober, paint regularly instead of when I felt like it. Now she's working on my cholesterol. When I'm perfect, which should be any day now, she'll probably dump me."

"I don't think so. So how'd you end up here?"

"Oh! I told her one day I had a fantasy of living on an island like Gauguin."

"You're kidding."

"I was. But she took me seriously. She said if she could find an island with good property values, we'd go. She did a lot of homework and we ended up here."

"You like it."

Dad smiles. "I love it."

Zack sighs. "You've got it all."

His father looks at him. "*Now* I have."

Zack blushes, looks down for a minute. "I had a pretty serious thing with a girl over the spring. But it's over now."

"Really? The one your mother mentioned last night?"

"Yeah."

"But she called you. Is it really over?"

"Sure."

His dad laughs. "You should have said yes, Zack. How many times do I have to tell you?"

At the same moment they both pick up their empty glasses and take a mouthful of ice to chew.

After lunch they cruise the shops, look first at Dad's semiserious paintings, then the serious ones. Zack admires his father's work. But he's also pleased it's different from his own. In one of the shops Dad buys a postcard o the island, a view of the lighthouse at night. "This is fo Eleanor," he explains.

"Eleanor?"

"I like to send her postcards and junk at her office. She sends me stuff at home. Sickening, huh?"

"No, it's pretty nice." Zack buys a postcard too. He thinks he might send it to Clara. Then again, he migh not. For a while he's just going to follow his impulses.

SEVENTEEN

Zack is in it up to his neck. At first, he stayed by the shoreline with Beamer, playing fetch the flip-flop. But then Zack felt the pull of the high seas and began walking cautiously toward Spain, testing to see how far he could go and still keep his feet.

A far cry from early this morning, when his father could hardly get him in the water. "I don't have a bathing suit!" Zack had protested.

"Sissy!" his father remarked, and walked away, leaving Zack on the deserted beach. It was a confusing moment. After all, he didn't fully know this man. Was he being rejected? Abandoned for all times because he wouldn't go in the water? He had stood hugging himself in the pre-dawn chill, waiting for further instructions. The beach was lovely at that hour, prettier than Fort Lauderdale Beach, which was flat and gritty and dominated by lines of parking meters. The sand here was white, tinted laven-der in the dawn, and there were softly rounded dunes and more of that graceful marsh grass, waving in the wind. This part of the beach was private, completely deserted. "People who live near the beach never go to the beach," his father had pointed out, and Zack knows it is true. He hasn't been to Fort Lauderdale Beach since he was a kid.

After a few scary minutes his father returned, holding aloft a big pair of shears. "Hold still," he said, kneeling on the sand in front of Zack.

"Wait!" Zack had screamed, needing to explain that these were his favorite jeans; they were perfectly soft and broken in, and had pockets just where he wanted them . . . But before he could form a sentence, he was wearing cutoffs.

"Now," his father said with satisfaction, "you've got a bathing suit!" And he was off, splashing into the surf in his little black Speedo, diving headlong into the waves like a dolphin. Beamer had run joyfully after him.

Leaving Zack staring down at his own bare legs and a pile of denim carnage in the sand. The scissors caught the rising sun and gleamed wickedly. Zack's first impulse was to follow his father into the water with the scissors and cut off something *he* was attached to, then suddenly he understood. He saw it his father's way. The jeans weren't as important as the moment. There would be millions of pairs of jeans in Zack's life but only one moment like this. He gave the denim on the sand a kick and ran into the cold salty water, laughing.

They played for hours, swimming, wrestling, throwing water on the dog and each other. Then Dad sloshed back to shore for a rest. He is stretched out flat in the sand now; a Panama hat covers his face.

But Zack is spellbound and can't leave the ocean. He

feels part of it. He is rocking and sparkling in perfect harmony with it. It is testing him to see how far from the shore he can walk without being afraid. He steps forward and water covers his mouth, stinging his lips with salt. His eyes are blinded by sun-dazzle. A wave is coming. This one will cover his head, perhaps take him off his feet. He waits for it, fearless, thrilled. The water rises and rises, rolling and curling above him like a canopy. Then down, soaking him, drenching his upturned face. His feet let go of the soft sand and he holds his breath for the plunge, the inversion, and the automatic bob back to the surface. He treads water, tipping his head back to gaze lovingly at the endless sky. This is the most blissful moment of his life.

He checks out the shoreline. Eleanor is finally up, and is threading her way down to the beach. On Saturdays she likes to sleep late.

Eleanor is wearing one of his father's blue shirts, with the sleeves rolled up. Her legs are bare. She goes to Zack's dad and kicks sand on him, to wake him up. He grabs her ankle and pulls her off her feet. They wrestle. Zack sees a flash of red bikini bottom. Then they get serious for a minute. Eleanor sort of holds his father down and kisses him. It goes on a long time.

Zack wants to be with them. He starts for shore making long even strokes with his arms and legs, loving the hard pull of exercise. By the time he splashes up on the beach, Eleanor and his father have become the picture of circumspection, sitting up in the sand side by side and sorting through mail. Eleanor is now wearing the Panama hat, along with some very sharp sunglasses. She looks up at Zack and waves something. A postcard!

His heart beats fast. This is from Clara. He had sent one to her earlier in the week; had agonized over the message for two hours. He wanted to write "I love you too," because of what she had said to him on the phone. But he didn't have the guts. Finally he settled for "Hello, New Jersey."

"You got mail!" Eleanor calls.

He approaches them, dripping and blushing, and takes the card. A picture of Fort Lauderdale Beach. He turns it over. *Hello, Kansas*. His wet hands are making the ink run. Zack feels a rush of love.

"Is it from that girl you aren't going with?" Dad asks.

"Mind your own business." Zack smiles.

"I'll keep it safe for you," Eleanor says, taking the card and tucking it into her little survival pack. "Your father might cut it up." She glances at the pile of denim and scissors nearby.

"I'll buy him a new pair!" Dad says. "He was hovering on the shoreline, afraid to get wet."

"You're lucky he didn't carry you out and dump you in the water," Eleanor tells Zack. "That's what he does with me."

Zack wishes he could see a demonstration of that.

"Speaking of correspondence," says Dad, drawing a line in the sand with his finger. "How about dropping a quick postcard on your mother? Just something simple. 'Having a wonderful time. Glad you're not here.' "

"I'm not ready," Zack says.

"I'm not saying you have to talk to her on the phone or anything, although I am getting royally sick of screening your calls."

Zack lowers his eyes. "It's not my fault she calls here every night. I just can't deal with her now, okay?"

"You have to deal with her," Dad says quietly. "She's your mother."

"Don't push him," Eleanor says.

"I'm supposed to push him. I'm his father. That's what fathers do. They push. Anyway, this one likes to be pushed."

"I do not!" Zack says hotly. "You just want me to go home because you're sick of having me here! Aren't you?"

"Bullshit!" his father shouts back. "You know better than that!"

"Hey! Hey!" Eleanor says. "Let's talk intelligently."

"Tell *him*!" Zack and his father say together. Then they laugh and it takes some of the edge off.

"All right," Dad says. "Let me just make a short speech, okay?"

"Now you did it," Eleanor mutters to Zack.

Zack's father glances at her, then looks at Zack. "All right. Now listen to me, Tiger. Really listen. If I could have my way, you'd stay here forever. Or at least for thirteen years to make up for the thirteen years I lost. I love having you here. I love you. Okay?"

"Okay," Zack mumbles.

"I like you too," Eleanor puts in.

"But the point is, Zachary, you have to learn to *deal* with your mother. You can't just run away and take vacations from her when it gets to be too much for you. You have to learn to look her in the eye and tell her what's what."

"You're dreaming," Zack says.

Dad shrugs. "If you can't do that, you'll never grow up. She'll have power over you forever."

"I know." Zack lowers his head like a scolded child.

"You certainly don't have any trouble asserting yourself with me," Dad points out. "What's the difference?"

Zack tries to think. "Well . . . I know if I lose it in front of you, you'll forgive me. I feel like, if I make the wrong move with her, she'll hate me forever."

"That's how she jerks people around, Tiger. You better learn to fight it or you'll spend the rest of your life basing all your decisions on what *she* might think."

Zack looks up, confused. "You make her sound like some kind of— She's a good person. She's had a hard time—"

"Everyone's had a hard time," Eleanor interjects. "But we don't use it as a weapon."

"Yeah," Zack says softly. He looks down the beach where Beamer is stalking some small creature, probably a crab.

"Look," Dad says. "Why don't you just call her and tell her you'd like to spend the rest of the summer here?"

"Could I?" Zack cries. "The whole summer?"

"Sure. But the price is, you have to tell her. Like a man."

"Oh. Can I think about that?"

Dad takes his hat from Eleanor and swats at Zack with it. "Hopeless!" he says affectionately.

Eleanor removes her shirt and chucks it aside. Then she takes a tube of sunscreen from her pack and begins to apply it to her neck and shoulders. Zack and his father both watch attentively. "I know what I'd do in your place, Zack," she says. "I'd get my own place in the fall. It can even be near your house, but I think you'd benefit from living on your own."

"What he should really do is go away to school," Dad says. "Like here, for instance. South Carolina has some wonderful universities."

"We decided it would be better for me to live at home and go to a community college," Zack explains.

"You and Mom decided?" Dad asks. "Or Mom decided?"

Zack looks up, harried. "I don't know!"

"Pushing, pushing," Eleanor says to Dad.

"Just tell me," Dad says. "Do you like the idea of a community college, or do you really secretly wish you could go away?"

Zack is short of breath. "Well, she had all these good reasons. Like she needs me to help around the house and cut the grass . . ."

"Is Joshua crippled?"

"And the money . . ."

"Money! That's not an issue and she knows it! I told her I would pay for anything and everything you wanted, up to Harvard and Yale."

The sun is almost overhead now, oppressively hot. "She knew that? She knew you would pay for anything?"

"Of course! What do you think I am? Frankly, I was surprised when she told me you wanted to live at home and commute. I mean, with your grades and your talent, you could write your own ticket."

Zack is almost panting from the heat. "She— I didn't know you existed then. I thought she'd have to pay for everything out of her savings, you know? It seemed only decent to offer to do the cheapest thing . . ."

"She didn't care what would be best for you, did she?" Dad says quietly. "She lied to you so you'd be tricked into doing what was best for her."

"No!" Zack shouts. "You can't say that about her! She's not like that!"

His father looks at him steadily. "Yes, she is."

"No!" Zack wants to cry. "You don't know her! I've been living with her, not you! You left! She's a good, sweet, self-sacrificing person! She'd do anything for me! She would!"

Dad raises his voice. "Don't you see this? Can't you see what she's done to you? You're afraid to question her or even do the slightest rebellious thing! For Pete's sake, what's wrong with you? Are you a complete wimp? Don't you have any of me in you at all?"

"You . . ." Zack sputters with rage. "How am I supposed to be anything like you? All the time I was growing up, when I needed you, you were gone!"

"That's *her* fault!"

"No! It's yours too! It's yours. You had to do this stupid thing of running off with me and that's how we lost each other. If you'd just gone away and divorced her like a normal person, you'd have had visitation rights and I could have had . . . all that time with you, but you never do anything the easy way, do you? You always have to be so fucking dramatic!" Zack is panting, shocked at himself but strangely proud.

His father just stares. Then he lowers his head. Zack realizes with horror he is struggling not to cry.

Eleanor jumps up. "I'll go and see about lunch," she says.

Zack touches his father's arm. "Daddy, I'm sorry," he says.

Dad shakes his head no. "It's okay," he says in a rough voice. "It's all right. What you said was true."

"But . . . it wasn't fair. You can't help being the way you are."

His father looks up. "That's right. And neither can your mom. And neither can you."

Zack takes a deep breath. "I think I want to go home and talk to her. There's some stuff I want to try to make her understand."

His father smiles faintly. "That's my Tiger."

•

For his farewell dinner they take him to a fancy restaurant in Shelter Cove called Harbourmaster's. His father has to lend him a jacket and tie for the occasion. Zack feels good in his dad's clothes. The jacket is almost a perfect fit, and he loves the tie, a navy and silver paisley. Later Dad tells him he can keep it.

Eleanor is the showpiece of the group, of course, in the definitive little black dress. Her hair is pulled up, and she wears tiny diamond studs in her ears. Very Grace Kelly. Inside the restaurant candlelight emphasizes the gold of her hair, the ivory skin, the strange combination of harshness and innocence in her blue eyes. Zack alternately gazes at her and watches his father gazing at her. His dad's expression is more awe than lust. Eleanor doesn't gaze back at Zack's dad, but she does subtle things. When he speaks, she looks down at her lap as if she were memorizing every word. Zack wonders if he and Clara will get to this point. He wonders if they will get anywhere at all.

The prices on the menu take his breath away, and involuntarily Zack thinks how much Mom would disapprove. He has been noting all week the many things about his father she would disapprove of. The frivolous spending, the goofing off, the frightening amounts of junk food. Eleanor herself—too sexy. Mom would say "too obvious." Not a lady. Even their hedge would be too bright and showy for her. A blossom here and there, in a nice, pale pink, but not this gaudy profusion.

Zack wonders if he agrees. His father's world is fun, but Zack has to admit he has begun to miss home cooking and regular hours. And his new blue jeans are *not* as good as the ones Dad destroyed. Still, he doesn't want to be like his mom, either, always buying a car for its gas mileage, always giving exact change to sales clerks, afraid to use a four-letter word. Zack knows the answer. He can't be either one of them. He has to settle who and what he is on an issue-by-issue basis. That's why he has to leave home. That's why everybody has to leave home.

But tonight it's Dad and Eleanor's world, and he loves being a guest there, watching Eleanor clink her champagne against Dad's mineral water, hearing Dad rattle off the names of French dishes as he orders the meal, eating food so pretty he hates to cut it up. The restaurant has glass walls and sits out in the marina, so they are surrounded by the dark sparkle of starlit water. That's what he'll remember about Hilton Head. Things sparkle here. Eleanor's earrings, crystal in firelight, his father's personality. Zack hopes he can take just a little of that sparkle back with him.

They talk only of pleasant things during dinner. They sip coffee as Zack tackles an evil dessert heaped with chocolate shavings. Now they begin to talk about tomorrow.

"Are you all packed?" Eleanor asks.

"Yeah." Zack almost chokes at the thought of going home. He is being sent into battle. A weird silent battle with weapons he doesn't understand. He gulps ice water. "I think I'll stay about a week. I want to see my girlfriend. And I need to get a recommendation from my art teacher for the institute." He has decided to apply to the Art Institute of Atlanta. It seems perfect. Halfway between Florida and South Carolina, excellent reputation, thriving arts community. And outside the city, woods and mountains to roam with Beamer. Dad and Eleanor both know Atlanta and can help him find a good place to live.

"We'll miss you, Tiger. But listen. If she wants you to spend more than a week with her . . ."

"No," Zack says. "I'm spending July and August with you guys. She kept me away from you all those years and I have the right to be with you now."

"That's my Tiger." Dad smiles.

Zack slumps. "It's real easy to be a tiger here. Back home I'll be a mouse in five minutes."

"You can do it," Dad says.

"I don't know." Zack sighs. "I wish I could take you with me."

His dad laughs. "Didn't you know? I am going with you."

He looks up. "Huh?"

His father smiles. "You take your parents with you wherever you go."

•

All too soon it's the next morning and Zack's car is loaded up and he's standing in the driveway with a champagne headache and a bad case of nerves. Beamer has chased Dandelion up a tree, so she'll have something to remember him by. He's now settled in the backseat, chewing on Zack's backpack.

Dad looks like he's going to cry or something. Everyone hesitates. Finally Eleanor moves, grabbing Zack and giving him a big hug. Then Zack goes and throws his arms around his father. They hold tight. Zack thinks of Dorothy, hugging the scarecrow. *I think I'll miss you most of all.*

Then he is in his car, rolling back out of the driveway. They are shouting advice from both sides. Dad, about standing up to people. Eleanor, about road safety.

Then they are just an attractive blond couple in the rearview mirror, waving good-bye against a hedge of flaming azaleas, getting smaller and smaller.

Zack concentrates on directions, getting himself off the island and onto the highway back to Hardeeville. The dark Carolina woods are even scarier in daylight than they were in darkness. The car is hot and silent except for Beamer who is panting in the backseat. Zack is all alone now, heading for the battle of his life, the battle for his life.

He doesn't feel like he's going to win.

EIGHTEEN

Zack cuts the engine, lets it die. Why does his house look strange? He has only been gone a week. Somehow it looks smaller. No one comes out on the porch to greet him, but he didn't exactly expect that anyway.

"We're home," he says to Beamer, stalling for time.

Beamer yawns. None of this is his problem.

Sweating and stiff, Zack climbs out of the car. He's hot. Florida is hotter than South Carolina. A trickle of sweat runs down his back when he reaches for his gear. He wishes he could go somewhere and take a shower before he has to face them.

"Tiger, tiger, burning bright," he chants to himself. It's become his prayer, his way of pretending to be braver than he is. He recited it to himself all the way down here, hoping it would bolster him. Last night at the truck stop in Jacksonville, he put himself to sleep with it. He called his mother from there, told her he'd be coming back this morning. Sunday morning. "We'll stay home from church then," she had said. Another sin for his scroll. When he woke in the morning and creaked into a McDonald's for breakfast, his poem had coded itself into his brain, play-

222

ing in the back of his mind like a song, telling him he's stronger than he thinks because he's Anthony Lloyd's son.

But he's Mary Lloyd's son, too, and just standing here on her porch, inhaling her bougainvillaea, makes him suddenly revert. He wants to be a good boy. He wants everything to be as simple and pleasant and cozy as it was before he had a personality.

He rings the bell like a stranger.

Josh opens the door. He looks different too. Older? Taller? No, that's impossible. It's just his serious expression.

"Hi."

"Hi."

Josh drops to his knees and hugs Beamer, clinging to his fur. He closes his eyes. He obviously wants to make Zack feel guilty for taking him away and disrupting things. That's the MO in this place. Don't say anything, just pull strings. Only now, at least, Zack can see it happening.

"Where's Mom?"

Josh stands up and his eyes bore into Zack's. "In her room. She'll be out in a minute. Have you had breakfast?"

"Yeah." Zack sits on the edge of a chair, wiping his palms on his knees.

Suddenly there she is in a doorway, in a lilac silk blouse. Her lovely blue eyes sparkle with tears. This is not what he expected. She comes toward him, holding her arms out. Automatically he rises for the embrace. Her arms circle him. Her cologne fills his head. *Mommy*.

"I'm so glad you came home," she says tearfully into his shoulder.

Zack isn't sure he likes this. Does she think he's back for good? That everything is solved? He stiffens a little in her arms. "We have to talk," he says.

She lets go. "Yes." She sits down in a chair and looks at him expectantly, like a child.

Zack glances at Josh who has fixed him with a murderous glare. *How can you hurt this sweet woman?* Zack looks back at his mother who now smiles through her tears. A funny phrase crosses his mind. *Good cop, bad cop*.

"How is your father?" she asks bravely.

"He's fine." Zack lifts his chin. "I really like him."

Josh snorts.

"Do you want to say something?" Zack demands sharply.

Josh lifts *his* chin. "No."

"Good."

Mom goes on manfully. "Is he still . . . living with that . . . *girl*?"

"Eleanor. Yes. She's nice too."

This gets a moment of silence. "Is he still drinking?"

"No. He's been sober for six years."

"I know that's what he *says*."

"It's true. I was there. He drank iced tea and mineral water. Their refrigerator was full of Kool-Aid."

"Well . . ." She smiles a little to herself.

Zack lets his anger push him forward. "I've asked if I can spend the rest of the summer with them."

Dead silence. Two stunned faces.

"What?" his mother says.

"You heard me. I like it there. I like spending time with him. He makes me feel . . . free."

"Oh, yes!" she says. "I'm sure he does."

"He's a good person. Don't run him down."

She sits back in her chair, folds her hands. "I was afraid this would happen."

"What?" Zack demands. "What?"

She looks at him calmly. "I know how he operates. He's so charming. He makes everyone feel special. For a while. But you'll find out. He just tells you what you want to hear. When he's tired of you—"

"What are you talking about?" Zack says. "That's *your* relationship with him. I'm his son. He's not going to get tired of me!"

"Well, when he does, I'll be here," she says quietly. "Good old dependable Mom. Maybe I'm not flashy. Maybe I don't make you feel *free*, but when you really need somebody to count on—"

"Mom! He admits he's made mistakes! I'm not saying he's perfect, but he's my father and there are some things I really love about him."

She sighs. "I guess you'll just have to learn the hard way."

"Mother," Zack interrupts. "Isn't it conceivable that I could have a relationship with you and with him?"

She sighs. "I can't stop you."

"That's right. You can't." Zack is already feeling tired, as if he had chopped a cord of wood. And they haven't even covered the big stuff.

"So!" she says brightly. "You just came here to do your laundry and then you'll be off again. Is that it?"

"No," Zack says evenly. "I want to talk about some other stuff too."

She waves her hands. "Well, go ahead! You can't say anything worse than you already have."

"I'm not going to BCC. I'm going to apply to the Art Institute of Atlanta and I think I can get in."

She sucks in air. "Atlanta, Georgia?"

"That's the one."

"Well, I *know* that's his idea. He spent years in Atlanta doing God knows what."

"It was *my* idea. I need to be in a big city for a couple of years. As an artist."

"Yes, I think I understand what you mean," she says cynically.

"You do not! You've never taken enough interest in what I do to know what I'm talking about! Atlanta has one of the best art museums in the South! They get the shows I need to see! They have galleries where you can see all the new things that are happening. They have all kinds of teachers in residence. I think I'm really good, Mom. I want to give myself the best possible chance. And also . . . I'm eighteen and I think it would be good if I lived on my own for a while."

"It's amazing. One week away and you sound just like him."

"Good! And another thing. He told me he offered to pay for any kind of education either of us wanted. It was sure nice of you to keep that from us. But I guess you were forced to, since you were trying to make us believe our father was *dead*. I'm sorry, Mom, but you need to think about what you did to me and Josh. You took our *father* away from us. You took away all those years I could have known him. Nobody can ever give that back to me! Never! So you'll have to excuse me now if I want to start doing things my way. Because your judgment doesn't impress me all that much! Okay?"

She looks at him stonily. "There's nothing I can say to you, Zachary. He's got you completely brainwashed. If you can really look me in the face and tell me I did a bad job raising you—"

"I didn't say that! In a lot of ways you were a perfect mother. But you were wrong to lie to us about Dad, and you were wrong to keep us from him. All I'm trying to do is fix that. I need him just as much as I need you, and if you don't like that, there's nothing I can do. But you can't stop me either."

She gets up suddenly. "You're right. I can't," she says, and walks out of the room.

Zack lets his breath out. He had hoped he could make her understand. Did she even listen to what he had said? He doesn't think so.

He looks up to see Joshua glaring at him. "Are you happy now?" he asks.

Zack bites his lip. "Don't you even want to know about Dad? Aren't you the least bit curious about your own father?"

Josh's eyes are cold. "I've already heard more about him than I want to. Look what he's done to you. You were never like this before. She's right about him. He's a trou-blemaker. Before you started remembering him, every-thing was fine. We were all happy!"

"*I* wasn't happy!" Zack cries. "Something's been wrong with me since the day he left. This past week it's been like I found a missing piece of myself. You don't have to feel that way, but that's how *I* feel. Okay?"

Josh rises for his exit. "Do what you want. You're noth-ing but a selfish bastard. We don't need you anyway."

"Josh!" Zack calls after him.

Josh stops and turns.

Zack looks steadily into his brother's eyes. "I don't give a rat's ass what you or anyone else thinks of me."

Josh gasps a little, then recovers and exits.

Zack closes his eyes. It was hard. It was painful. But for once he had said exactly what he was feeling.

•

Next on the agenda is Clara. Zack has called her, told her he wants to come over and have a serious talk. She says she thinks that's a good idea. Driving over, Zack practices his speech.

228

All right. I know you had a very upsetting relationship before. I can't even imagine what that was like. But you were wrong to expect me to fix that for you. You said you were attracted to me because I seemed calm and stable. If I look that way it's because I've been stuffing my feelings all my life. That was the only way I could survive my childhood. My mom wanted kids who were calm and stable, so I learned to give her what she wanted. But that's not really me. Right now I'm full of all kinds of emotions because I have to learn all my feelings from scratch, like a baby. You're worried because I'm in therapy. Well, too bad. I need it. It's making me feel better and I'm through apologizing for not being what everybody wants. I think right now I'm kind of a moody, mixed-up person who doesn't know what he's feeling. If you want something safer, go look for it. But I'm really trying my best, and if you could just be patient with me, I think we could really have something good.

He sighs. She'll never let him get through something that long without interruptions. He'll have to pare it down.

He pulls into her driveway, shaking badly. The front door opens. She comes out. She is wearing one of the sundresses he loves, the pink and white seersucker. She's more beautiful than he remembered. Eyes like a doe. Body . . . legs . . . He feels dizzy.

She runs to him and pulls open the passenger door, climbing in with a rustle of skirts. She is barefoot. Her legs are tan. There's a Band-Aid on one toe. Lilac scent sweeps over him, unlocking memories.

Tears stand in her eyes, wetting the lashes. Zack realizes that somehow they have already had the whole conversation he was planning. She knows he's a problem child. But here she is anyway. He puts his arms around her, hugging, crushing. Then he gives a much shorter version of his speech. "I love you too."

•

"Well, well, well, well, well, well, well!" Nancy crushes out her cigarette and starts a new one. "I go out of town for two weeks, trying to have a life, and what happens? You get your memory back. You reunite with your father. You make your appropriate adolescent break from your mother. You begin to assert your own identity and you reconcile with your girlfriend. The only conclusion I can come to is that I was holding you back!"

Zack laughs. "No, I don't think so. I think I got the lid off the jar because you've been in there hitting it with a knife and running hot water on it all this time."

She grabs a pencil and scratch pad. "I like that. I'm going to steal that and use it the next time I give a seminar."

He giggles. "So what should we work on now?"

She looks up. "Now? We work on nothing. I work on your final invoice. Then we shake and you go off to college."

"No, wait!" he cries. "I still need you. My life is a mess now. My family won't even speak to me. My house is like a pit full of rattlesnakes."

"Well, that's because you're acting differently than you ever did before. They're not used to hearing you assert yourself. You have to give them time to adjust."

Zack lowers his head. "But Mom's never going to forgive me, is she?"

Nancy smiles. "She loves you, Zack. Most of the crazy things she did were just misguided love. You have to realize how scared she is. She thinks you're choosing your father over her—"

"But I'm not! I want them both!"

"Well, let her know that. Reassure her. Spend an extra week here before you go back to your dad. Ask her advice about something. Anything. Just make her feel like she's still your mom. See?"

"I'll try. What about Josh?"

"Well, he's being loyal to her. Just win her over and he'll fall into line. I'm not saying this will be easy, but it will resolve itself. Someday Joshua will want to meet his father and you're the one he'll ask about it."

"Oh, no, he said—"

"Zack, don't pay any attention to anything people say. People say all kinds of things. Give your family a chance to change their minds. That's the kindest thing you can do for people. Now, have you got any other problems before I slam your file shut and kick your ass out the door?"

"I don't think you understand. I've got a million problems. I mean, there's the stuff with Mom and then I'm also sort of uncomfortable with Dad, because it's like I know him, but in a lot of ways he's a stranger. And I don't know if I really want to get serious with Clara. And I'm scared to go away to school in the fall."

"All that sounds like a normal eighteen-year-old to me. I have to reserve my time for people with serious problems."

"You're just dumping me!"

She crushes out her cigarette and leans forward. "Zack. Your main problem wasn't nightmares. It was co-dependence. You lived and died to please your mother. You even erased your memory for her. If I don't kick you out of the nest right now, you'll just shift that dependency to me. And I'll tell you a secret. I like you so much, I'd enjoy that. So you've definitely got to go."

"Well . . ." Zack thinks desperately. "What if my nightmares come back? They could. I don't even remember what I dreamed last night. Maybe I'm having nightmares so terrible I can't even remember them!"

She laughs. "You're really full of shit, Zack. I'm going to miss that."

He grins. "I think I get that from my father."

She holds out her hand. "Good luck at the Art Institute."

He knows it's hopeless. He stands up. "Good-bye, Nancy." He pauses at the door. "And thank you."

She waggles her fingers at him. "Sweet dreams, Tiger!"